ANDREA CAMILLERI

THE VOICE OF THE VIOLIN

Translated by Stephen Sartarelli

PICADOR

First published 2003 by Viking Penguin,
a member of Penguin Putnam Inc., New York

First published in Great Britain 2005 by Picador
an imprint of Pan Macmillan Ltd
Pan Macmillan, 20 New Wharf Road, London N1 9RR
Basingstoke and Oxford
Associated companies throughout the world
www.panmacmillan.com

ISBN 0 330 49298 5 HB
ISBN 0 330 49300 0 TPB

3 5 7 9 8 6 4 2

A CIP catalogue record for this book is available from
the British Library.

Typeset by SetSystems Ltd, Saffron Walden, Essex
Printed and bound in Great Britain by
Mackays of Chatham plc, Chatham, Kent

THE VOICE OF THE VIOLIN

ONE

Inspector Salvo Montalbano could immediately tell that it was not going to be his day the moment he opened the shutters of his bedroom window. It was still night, at least an hour before sunrise, but the darkness was already lifting, enough to reveal a sky covered by heavy rain clouds and, beyond the light strip of beach, a sea that looked like a Pekingese dog. Ever since a tiny dog of that breed, all decked out in ribbons, had bitten painfully into his calf after a furious fit of hacking that passed for barking, Montalbano saw the sea this way whenever it was whipped up by crisp, cold gusts into thousands of little waves capped by ridiculous plumes of froth. His mood darkened, especially considering that an unpleasant obligation awaited him that morning. He had to attend a funeral.

*

The previous evening, finding some fresh anchovies cooked by Adelina, his houskeeper, in the fridge, he'd dressed

3

them in a great deal of lemon juice, olive oil and freshly ground black pepper, and wolfed them down. And he'd relished them, until it was all spoiled by a telephone call.

'H'lo, Chief? Izzatchoo onna line?'

'It's really me, Cat. You can go ahead and talk.'

At the station they'd given Catarella the job of answering the phone, mistakenly thinking he could do less damage there than anywhere else. After getting mightily pissed off a few times, Montalbano had come to realize that the only way to talk to him within tolerable limits of nonsense was to use the same language as he.

'Beckin' pardon, Chief, for the 'sturbance.'

Uh-oh. He was begging pardon for the disturbance. Montalbano pricked up his ears. Whenever Catarella's speech became ceremonious, it meant there was no small matter at hand.

'Get to the point, Cat.'

'Tree days ago somebody aks for you, Chief, wanted a talk t' you in poisson, but you wasn't 'ere an' I forgotta reference it to you.'

'Where were they calling from?'

'From Florida, Chief.'

Montalbano was literally overcome with terror. In a flash he saw himself in a sweatsuit jogging alongside fearless, athletic American narcotics agents working with him on a complicated investigation into drug trafficking.

'Tell me something. What language did you speak with them?'

'What langwitch was I asposta speak? We spoke 'Talian, Chief.'

'Did they tell you what they wanted?'

'Sure, they tol' me everyting about one ting. They said as how Vice Commissioner Tamburrano's wife was dead.'

Montalbano breathed a sigh of relief, he couldn't help it. They'd called not from Florida, but from police headquarters in the town of Floridia near Siracusa. Caterina Tamburrano had been gravely ill for some time, and the news was not a complete surprise to him.

'Chief, izzat still you there?'

'Still me, Cat, I haven't changed.'

'They also said the obsequious was gonna be on Tuesday morning at nine o'clock.'

'Thursday? You mean tomorrow morning?'

'Yeah, Chief.'

He was too good a friend of Michele Tamburrano not to go to the funeral. That way he could make up for not having even phoned to express his condolences. Floridia was about a three-and-a-half-hour drive from Vigàta.

'Listen, Cat, my car's in the garage. I need a squad car at my place, in Marinella, at five o'clock sharp tomorrow morning. Tell Inspector Augello I'll be out of the office until early afternoon. Got that?'

*

He emerged from the shower, skin red as a lobster. To counteract the chill he felt at the sight of the sea, he'd made the water too hot. As he started shaving, he heard the squad car arrive. Indeed, who, within a ten-kilometre radius, hadn't heard it? It rocketed into the drive at supersonic speed, braked with a scream, firing bursts of gravel in every direction, then followed this display with a roar of the racing engine, a harrowing shift of gears, a shrill screech of skidding tyres, and another explosion of gravel. The driver had executed an evasive manoeuvre, turning the car completely round.

When Montalbano stepped out of the house ready to leave, he saw Gallo, the station's official driver, rejoicing.

'Look at that, Chief! Look at them tracks! What a manoeuvre! A perfect one-eighty!'

'Congratulations,' Montalbano said gloomily.

'Should I put on the siren?' Gallo asked as they were about to set out.

'Put it in your arse,' said a surly Montalbano, closing his eyes. He didn't feel like talking.

*

Gallo, who suffered from the Indianapolis Complex, stepped on the accelerator as soon as he saw his superior's eyes shut, reaching a speed he thought better suited to his driving ability. They'd been on the road barely fifteen minutes when the crash occurred. At the scream of the brakes, Montalbano opened his eyes but saw nothing, head lurching violently forward before being jerked back by the safety belt. Next came a deafening clang of metal against metal, then silence again, a fairy-tale silence, with birds singing and dogs barking.

'You hurt?' the inspector asked Gallo, seeing him rub his chest.

'No. You?'

'Nothing. What happened?'

'A chicken ran in front of me.'

'I've never seen a chicken run in front of a car before. Let's look at the damage.'

They got out. There wasn't a soul about. The long skid marks were etched into the tarmac. Right at the spot where they began, you could see a small, dark stain. Gallo went up to it, then turned triumphantly around.

'What did I tell you?' he said to the inspector. 'It was a chicken!'

A clear case of suicide. The car they had slammed into, smashing up its entire rear end, must have been legally parked at the side of the road, though now it was sticking out slightly. It was a bottle-green Renault Twingo, positioned so as to block a unpaved drive leading to a two-storey house with shuttered windows and doors some thirty metres away. The squad car, for its part, had a shattered headlight and a crumpled right bumper.

'So now what do we do?' Gallo asked dejectedly.

'We're going to go on. Will the car run, in your opinion?'

'I'll give it a try.'

Reversing with a great clatter of metal, the squad car

dislodged itself from the other vehicle. Nobody came to the windows of the house. They must have been fast asleep, dead to the world. The Twingo had to belong to someone in there, since there were no other homes in the immediate area. As Gallo was trying with his bare hands to bend out the bumper, which was scraping against the tyre, Montalbano wrote down the phone number of the Vigàta police headquarters on a piece of paper and slipped this under the Twingo's windscreen wiper.

☆

When it's not your day, it's not your day. After they'd been back on the road for half an hour or so, Gallo started rubbing his chest again, and from time to time he twisted his face in a grimace of pain.

'I'll drive,' said the inspector. Gallo didn't protest.

When they were outside the town of Fela, Montalbano, instead of continuing along the main road, turned onto the road that led to the centre of town. Gallo paid no attention, eyes closed and head resting against the window.

'Where are we?' he asked, as soon as he felt the car come to a halt.

'We're at Fela Hospital. Get out.'

'But it's nothing, Inspector!'

'Get out. I want them to have a look at you.'

'Well, just leave me here and keep going. You can pick me up on the way back.'

'Cut the shit. Let's go.'

Between auscultations, three blood pressure exams, X-rays, and everything else in the book, it took them over three hours to have a look at Gallo. In the end they ruled that he hadn't broken anything; the pain he felt was from having bumped hard into the steering wheel, and the weakness was a natural reaction to the fright he'd had.

'So now what do we do?' Gallo asked again, more dejected than ever.

'What do you think? We keep going. But I'll drive.'

*

The inspector had been to Floridia three or four times before. He even remembered where Tamburrano lived, and so he headed towards the Church of the Madonna delle Grazie, which was practically next door to his colleague's house. When they reached the square, he saw the church hung with black and a throng of people hurrying inside. The service must have started late. Apparently he wasn't the only one to have things go wrong.

'I'll take the car to the police garage in town and have them look at it,' said Gallo. 'I'll come and pick you up afterwards.'

Montalbano entered the crowded church. The service had just begun. He looked around and recognized no one. Tamburrano must have been in the first row, near the coffin in front of the main altar. The inspector decided to remain where he was, near the entrance. He would shake

Tamburrano's hand when the coffin was being carried out of the church. When the priest finally opened his mouth after the Mass had been going on for some time, Montalbano gave a start. He'd heard right, he was sure of it.

The priest had begun with the words, 'Our dearly beloved Nicola has left this vale of tears . . .'

Mustering up the courage, he tapped a little old lady on the shoulder.

'Excuse me, signora, whose funeral is this?'

'The dear departed Ragioniere Pecoraro. Why?'

'I thought it was for the Signora Tamburrano.'

'Ah, no, that one was at the Church of Sant'Anna.'

It took him almost fifteen minutes to get to the church of Sant'Anna, practically running the whole way. Panting and sweaty, he found the priest in the deserted nave.

'I beg your pardon. Where's the funeral of Signora Tamburrano?'

'That ended almost two hours ago,' said the priest, looking him over sternly.

'Do you know if she's being buried here?' Montalbano asked, avoiding the priest's gaze.

'Most certainly not. When the service was over, she was taken in the hearse to Vibo Valentia, where she'll be entombed in the family vault. Her bereaved husband followed behind in his car.'

So it had all been for naught. He had noticed, in the Piazza della Madonna delle Grazie, a cafe with tables outside. When Gallo returned, with the car repaired as well as could be expected, it was almost two o'clock. Montalbano told him what happened.

'So now what do we do?' Gallo asked for the third time, lost in an abyss of dejection.

'You're going to eat a brioche with a *granita di caffè*, which they make very well here, and then we'll head home. With the Good Lord's help and the Blessed Virgin's company, we should be back in Vigàta by evening.'

*

Their prayer was answered, the drive home smooth as silk.

'The car's still there,' said Gallo when Vigàta was already visible in the distance.

The Twingo was exactly the way they'd left it that morning, sticking slightly out from the top of the unpaved drive.

'They've probably already called headquarters,' said Montalbano.

He was bullshitting: the look of the car and the house with its shuttered windows made him uneasy.

'Turn back,' he suddenly ordered Gallo.

Gallo made a reckless U-turn that triggered a chorus of horn blasts. When they reached the Twingo, he executed another, even more reckless, then pulled up behind the damaged car.

Montalbano stepped out in a hurry. What he thought he'd just seen in the rear-view mirror, when passing by, turned out to be true: the scrap of paper with the telephone number was still under the windscreen wiper. Nobody'd touched it.

'I don't like it,' the inspector said to Gallo, who was now standing next to him. He started walking down the drive. The house must have been recently built; the grass in front was still burned from the lime. There was also a stack of new tiles in a corner of the yard. Montalbano carefully examined the shuttered windows. No light was filtering out.

He went up to the front door and rang the doorbell. He waited a short while, then rang again.

'Do you know whose house this is?'

'No, Chief.'

What should he do? Night was falling and he could feel the beginnings of fatigue. Their pointless, exhausting day was starting to weigh on him.

'Let's go,' he said. Then he added, in a vain attempt at convincing himself, 'I'm sure they called.'

Gallo gave him a doubtful look, but didn't open his mouth.

*

Gallo wasn't even invited into headquarters. The inspector had sent him immediately home to rest. His second-in-command, Mimì Augello, wasn't in; he'd been summoned to report to the new commissioner of Montelusa, Luca Bonetti-Alderighi, a young and testy native of Bergamo who in the course of one month had succeeded in creating knife-blade antipathies all around him.

'The commissioner was upset you weren't in Vigàta,' said Fazio, the sergeant he was closest to. 'So Inspector Augello had to go in your place.'

'*Had* to go?' the inspector retorted. 'He probably just saw it as a chance to show off!'

He told Fazio about their accident that morning and asked him if he knew who owned the house. Fazio didn't, but promised his superior that he'd go to the town hall the following morning and find out.

'By the way, your car's in our garage.'

Before going home, the inspector interrogated Cata-rella.

'Try hard to remember. Did anyone happen to call about a car we ran into?'

No calls.

*

'Let me try and understand a minute,' Livia said angrily by phone from Boccadasse, Genoa.

'What's to understand, Livia? As I said, and now repeat, François's adoption papers aren't ready yet. Some unexpected problems have come up, and I no longer have the old commissioner behind me always smoothing everything out. We have to be patient.'

'I wasn't talking about the adoption,' Livia said icily.

'You weren't? Then what were you talking about?'

'Getting married, that's what. We can certainly get married while the problems of the adoption are being worked out. The one thing does not depend on the other.'

'No, of course not,' said Montalbano, who was beginning to feel harried and cornered.

'Now I want a straight answer to the following question,' Livia went on, implacably. 'Supposing the adoption isn't possible: what will we do? Will we get married anyway, in your opinion, or won't we?'

A sudden, loud thunderclap gave him a way out.

'What was that?'

'Thunder. There's a terrible stor—'

He hung up and pulled out the plug.

*

He couldn't sleep. He tossed and turned, snarling himself up in the sheets. Around two in the morning, he realized it was useless. He got up, got dressed, grabbed a leather bag given to him some time ago by a house burglar who'd become his friend, got in his car and drove off. The storm was raging worse than ever; lightning bolts illuminated the sky. When he reached the Twingo, he slipped his car in under some trees and turned off the headlights. From the glove compartment he extracted a gun, a pair of gloves and a torch. After waiting for the rain to let up, he crossed the road in one bound, went up the drive and flattened himself against the front door. He rang and rang the doorbell but got no answer. He then put on the gloves and pulled a large key ring with a dozen or so variously shaped picklocks out of the leather bag. The door opened on the third try. It was locked with only the latch and hadn't been dead-bolted. He entered, closing the door behind him. In the dark, he bent over, untied his wet shoes and removed them, keeping his socks on. He turned on the torch, keeping it pointed at the ground. He found himself in a large dining room that opened onto a living room. The furniture smelled of varnish. Everything was new, clean and orderly. A door led into a kitchen that sparkled like something one might see in an advertisement; another door gave onto a bathroom so shiny it looked as if no one had ever used it before. He slowly climbed the stairs to the upper floor. There he found three closed doors. The first one he opened revealed a neat little guest room; the second led into a bigger bathroom than the one downstairs, but unlike it, this one was decidedly messy. A pink towelling bathrobe lay rumpled on the floor, as though the person wearing it had taken it off in a hurry. The third door was to the master bedroom. And the naked, half-kneeling female body, belly resting against the edge of the bed, arms spread, face buried in the sheet that the young, blonde woman had torn to shreds with her fingernails in the final throes of her death by suffocation, must have belonged to the owner of the house.

Montalbano went up to the corpse and, removing a glove, touched it lightly: it was cold and stiff. She must

have been very beautiful. The inspector went back downstairs, put his shoes back on, wiped up the wet spot they
had made on the floor, went out of the house, closed the
door, crossed the road, got in his car and left. His thoughts
were racing as he drove back to Marinella. How to have
the crime discovered? He certainly couldn't go and tell
the judge what he'd been up to. The judge who'd replaced
Lo Bianco – on a leave of absence to pursue his endless
historical research into the lives of a pair of unlikely
ancestors – was a Venetian by the name of Nicolò
Tommaseo who was always talking about his 'irrevocable
prerogatives'. He had a little baby face that he hid under
a Belfiore martyr's moustache and beard. As Montalbano
was opening the door to his house, the solution to the
problem finally came to him in a flash. And thus he was
able to enjoy a brief but god-like sleep.

TWO

He arrived at the office at eight thirty the next morning, looking rested and crisp.

'Did you know our new commissioner is noble?' was the first thing Mimì Augello said when he saw him.

'Is that a moral judgement or a heraldic fact?'

'Heraldic.'

'I'd already worked out as much from the little dash between his last names. And what did you do, Mimì? Did you call him count, baron or marquis? Did you butter him up nicely?'

'Come on, Salvo, you're obsessed!'

'Me? Fazio told me you were wagging your tail the whole time you were talking on the phone to the commissioner, and that afterwards you shot out of here like a rocket to go and see him.'

'Listen, the commissioner said, and I quote: "If Inspector Montalbano is not available, come here at once yourself." What was I supposed to do? Tell him I couldn't because my superior would get pissed off?'

'What did he want?'

'He wasn't alone. Half the province was there. He informed us he intended to modernize, to renovate. He said anyone unable to come up to speed with him should just hang it up. Those were his exact words: hang it up. It was clear to everyone he meant you and Sandro Turri of Calascibetta.'

'Explain to me how you knew this.'

'Because when he said "hang it up" he looked right at Turri and then at me.'

'Couldn't that mean he was actually referring to you?'

'Come on, Salvo, everybody knows he doesn't have a high opinion of you.'

'And what did his lordship want?'

'To tell us that in a few days, some absolutely up-to-date computers will be arriving. Every headquarters in the province will be equipped with them. He wanted each of us to give him the name of an officer we thought had a special knack for computer science. Which I did.'

'Are you insane? Nobody here knows a damn thing about that stuff. Whose name did you give him?'

'Catarella,' said an utterly serious Mimì Augello.

The act of a born saboteur. Montalbano stood up

abruptly, ran over to his second-in-command and embraced him.

✻

'I know all about the house you were interested in,' said Fazio, sitting down in the chair in front of the inspector's desk. 'I spoke to the town clerk, who knows everything about everyone in Vigàta.'

'Let's have it.'

'Well, the land the house was built on used to belong to a Dr Rosario Licalzi.'

'What kind of doctor?'

'A real one, a medical doctor. He died about fifteen years ago, leaving the plot to his eldest son, Emanuele, also a doctor.'

'Does he live in Vigàta?'

'No. He lives and works in Bologna. Two years ago, this Emanuele Licalzi married a girl from those parts. They came to Sicily on their honeymoon. The minute the lady saw the land she got it into her head that she would build a little house on it. And there you have it.'

'Any idea where the Licalzis are right now?'

'The husband's in Bologna. The lady was last seen in Vigàta three days ago, running around town trying to furnish the house. She drives a bottle-green Renault Twingo.'

'The one Gallo crashed into.'

'Right. The clerk told me she's not the kind of woman to go unnoticed. Apparently she's very beautiful.'

'I don't understand why she hasn't called yet,' said Montalbano, who, when he put his mind to it, could be a tremendous actor.

'I've formed my own theory about that,' said Fazio. 'The clerk said the lady's, well, really friendly – I mean, she's got a lot of friends.'

'Girlfriends?'

'And boyfriends,' Fazio said emphatically. 'It's possible she's staying with a family somewhere. Maybe they came and picked her up with their own car and she won't notice the damage till she gets back.'

'Sounds plausible,' concluded Montalbano, continuing his performance.

*

As soon as Fazio left, the inspector called up Clementina Vasile Cozzo.

'My dear lady, how are you?'

'Inspector! What a lovely surprise! I'm getting along all right, by the grace of God.'

'Mind if I drop in to say hello?'

'You are welcome to come whenever you like.'

Clementina Vasile Cozzo was an elderly paraplegic, a former elementary school teacher blessed with intelligence and endowed with a natural, quiet dignity. The inspector had met her during the course of a complex investigation some three months back and remained as attached to her as a son. Though Montalbano didn't openly admit it to himself, she was the sort of woman he wished he could have as a mother, having lost his own when he was too young to retain much memory of her beyond a kind of golden luminescence.

'Was Mama blonde?' he'd once asked his father in an attempt to explain to himself why his only image of her consisted of a luminous nuance.

'Like wheat in sunlight,' was his father's laconic reply.

Montalbano had got in the habit of calling on Signora Clementina at least once a week. He would tell her about whatever investigation he happened to be involved in, and the woman, grateful for the visit, which broke the monotony of her daily routine, would invite him to stay for dinner. Pina, the signora's housekeeper, was a surly type and, to make matters worse, she didn't like Montalbano. She did, however, know how to cook some exquisite, disarmingly simple dishes.

*

Signora Clementina, dressed rather smartly with an Indian silk shawl around her shoulders, showed him into the living room.

'There's a concert today,' she whispered, 'but it's almost over.'

Four years ago, Signora Clementina had learned from

her maid, Pina – who for her part had heard it from Yolanda, the violinist's housekeeper – that the illustrious Maestro Cataldo Barbera, who lived in the flat directly above hers, was in serious trouble with his taxes. So she'd discussed the matter with her son, who worked at the Montelusa Revenue Office, and the problem, which had essentially arisen from a mistake, was resolved. Some ten days later, the housekeeper Yolanda had brought her a note that said: 'Dear Signora. To repay you, though only in part, I will play for you every Friday morning from nine thirty to ten thirty. Yours very sincerely, Cataldo Barbera.'

And so every Friday morning, she would get all dressed up to pay homage to the Maestro in turn, and she would go and sit in a small sort of parlour where one could best hear the music. At exactly half past nine, on the floor above, the Maestro would strike up the first notes.

Everyone in Vigàta knew about Maestro Cataldo Barbera, but very few had ever seen him in person. Son of a railwayman, the future Maestro had drawn his first breath sixty-five years earlier in Vigàta, but left town before the age of ten when his father was transferred to Catania. The Vigatese had had to learn of his career from the newspapers. After studying violin, Cataldo Barbera had very quickly become an internationally renowned concert performer. Inexplicably, however, at the height of his fame, he had retired to Vigàta, where he bought an apartment and now lived in voluntary seclusion.

'What's he playing?' Montalbano asked.

Signora Clementina handed him a sheet of squared paper. On the day before the performance, the Maestro would customarily send her the programme, written out in pencil. The pieces to be played that day were Pablo de Sarasate's 'Spanish Dance', and the 'Scherzo-Tarantella', op. 16, of Henryk Wieniawski. When the performance was over, Signora Clementina plugged in the telephone, dialled a number, set the receiver down on a shelf and started clapping. Montalbano joined in with gusto. He knew nothing about music, but he was certain of one thing: Cataldo Barbera was a great artist.

'Signora,' the inspector began, 'I must confess that this is a self-interested visit on my part. I need you to do me a favour.'

He went on to tell her everything that had happened to him the previous day: the accident, going to the wrong funeral, his secret, night-time visit to the house, his discovery of the corpse. When he had finished, the inspector hesitated. He didn't quite know how to phrase his request.

Signora Clementina, who had felt by turns amused and disturbed by his account, urged him on.

'Go on, Inspector, don't be shy. What is it you want from me?'

'I'd like you to make an anonymous telephone call,' Montalbano said in a single breath.

*

He'd been back in the office about ten minutes when Catarella passed him a call from Dr Lattes, the commissioner's cabinet chief.

'Hello, Montalbano, old friend, how's it going? Eh, how's it going?'

'Fine,' Montalbano said curtly.

'I'm so happy to hear it,' the chief of the cabinet said snappily, true to the nickname of Caffè-Lattes that someone had hung on him for the dangerously cloying warmth of his manner.

'At your service,' Montalbano egged him on.

'Well, not fifteen minutes ago a woman called the switchboard asking to speak personally to the commissioner. She was very insistent. The commissioner, however, was busy and asked me to take the call. The woman was in hysterics, screaming that a crime had been committed at a house in the Tre Fontane district. Then she hung up. The commissioner would like you to go there, just to make sure, and then report back to him. The lady also said that the house is easy to spot because there's a bottle-green Twingo parked in front.'

'Oh my God!' said Montalbano, launching into the second act of his role, now that Signora Clementina had recited her part so perfectly.

'What is it?' Dr Lattes asked, his curiosity aroused.

'An amazing coincidence!' said Montalbano, his voice full of wonder. 'I'll tell you later.'

✻

'Hello? Inspector Montalbano here. Am I speaking to Judge Tommaseo?'

'Yes, good day. What can I do for you?'

'Your Honour, the chief of the commissioner's cabinet just informed me that they have received an anonymous phone call reporting a crime in a small house on the outskirts of Vigàta. He ordered me to go and have a look. And I'm going.'

'Might it not be some kind of tasteless practical joke?'

'Anything is possible. I simply wanted to let you know, out of respect for your prerogatives.'

'Yes, of course,' said Judge Tommaseo, pleased.

'Do I have your authorization to proceed?'

'Of course. And if a crime was indeed committed, I want you to notify me at once and wait for me to get there.'

Montalbano called Fazio, Gallo and Galluzzo and told them to come with him to the Tre Fontane district to see if a murder had been committed.

'At the same house you asked me for information about?' asked Fazio, dumbfounded.

'The same one where we crashed into the Twingo?' Gallo chimed in, eyeing his superior in amazement.

'Yes,' the inspector answered both, trying to look humble.

'What a nose, Chief!' Fazio cried out in admiration.

*

They had barely set out when Montalbano already felt fed up. Fed up with the farce he would have to act out, pretending to be surprised when they found the corpse, fed up with the time he would have to waste on the judge, the coroner and the forensics team, who were capable of taking hours before arriving at the crime scene. He decided to speed things up.

'Pass me the mobile phone,' he said to Galluzzo, who was sitting in front of him. Gallo, naturally, was at the wheel.

He punched in Judge Tommaseo's number.

'Montalbano here. Listen, Judge, that was no joke, that phone call. Sorry to say, we found a dead body in the house. A woman.'

There were different reactions among those present in the car. Gallo swerved into the oncoming lane, brushed against a truck loaded with iron rods, cursed, then regained control. Galluzzo gave a start, opened his eyes wide, twisted around and looked at his boss with his mouth agape. Fazio visibly stiffened and stared straight ahead, expressionless.

'I'll be right there,' said Judge Tommaseo. 'Tell me exactly where the house is.'

Increasingly fed up, Montalbano passed the mobile phone to Gallo.

'Explain to him where we're going. Then call Pasquano and the crime lab.'

Fazio didn't open his mouth until the car came to a stop behind the bottle-green Twingo.

'Did you put gloves on before you went in?' he asked.

'Yeah,' said Montalbano.

'Anyway, now that we're going in, touch everything as much as you want, just to be safe. Leave as many fingerprints as you can.'

'I'd already thought of that,' said the inspector.

After the storm of the previous night, there was very little left of the scrap of paper tucked under the windscreen wiper. The water had washed away the telephone number. Montalbano didn't bother to remove it.

*

'You two have a look around down here,' the inspector said to Gallo and Galluzzo.

Then, followed by Fazio, he went upstairs. With the light on, the dead woman's body upset him less than the night before, when he'd seen it only by the beam of the torch. It seemed less real, though certainly not fake. Livid, white and stiff, the corpse resembled those plaster casts of the victims of Pompeii. Face down as she was, it was impossible to see what she looked like, but her struggle against death must have been fierce. Clumps of blonde hair lay scattered over the torn sheet, and purplish bruises stood out across her shoulders and just below the nape of her neck. The killer must have had to use every bit of his strength to force her face so far down into the mattress that not a wisp of air could get through.

Gallo and Galluzzo came upstairs.

'Everything seems in order downstairs,' said Gallo.

True, she looked like a plaster cast, but she was still a young woman, murdered, naked, and in a position that suddenly seemed unbearably obscene to him, her most intimate privacy violated, thrown open by the eight eyes of the policemen in the room. As if to give her back some semblance of personhood and dignity, he asked Fazio, 'Did they tell you her name?'

'Yes. If that's Mrs Licalzi, her name was Michela.'

He went into the bathroom, picked the pink bathrobe up off the floor, brought it into the bedroom, and covered the body with it.

He went downstairs. Had she lived, Michela Licalzi would still have had some work to do to sort out the house.

In the living room, propped up in a corner, were two rolled-up rugs; the sofa and armchairs were still factory-wrapped in clear plastic; a small table lay upside down, legs up, on top of a big, unopened box. The only thing in any kind of order was a small glass display cabinet with the usual sorts of things carefully arranged inside: two antique fans, a few ceramic statuettes, a closed violin case and two very beautiful shells, collector's items.

The forensics team were the first to arrive. To replace the old chief of the crime lab, Jacomuzzi, Commissioner Bonetti-Alderighi had hand-picked the young Dr Arquà, who'd moved down from Florence. More than chief of forensics, Jacomuzzi had been an incurable exhibitionist, always the first to strike a pose for the photographers, TV cameramen and journalists. To rib him, as he often did, Montalbano used to call him 'Pippo Baudo'. Deep down, Jacomuzzi never believed much in forensics as a useful tool in investigations; he maintained that sooner or later intuition and reason would find the solution, with or without the support of microscopes and analyses. Heresies, to Bonetti-Alderighi, who quickly got rid of him. Vanni Arquà, for his part, was a dead ringer for Harold Lloyd. Hair always dishevelled, he dressed like an absent-minded professor from a thirties movie and worshipped science. Montalbano didn't care much for him, and Arquà repaid him in kind with cordial antipathy.

Forensics thus showed up in full force, in two cars with sirens screaming as if they were in Texas. There were eight of them, all in civvies, and the first thing they did was unload boxes and crates from the boots, looking like a film crew ready to start shooting. When Arquà walked into the living room, Montalbano didn't even say hello; he merely pointed his thumb upward, signalling that what concerned them was upstairs.

They hadn't all finished climbing the stairs before Montalbano heard Arquà's voice call out:

'Excuse me, Inspector, would you come up here a minute?'

He took his time. When he entered the bedroom, he felt the crime lab chief's eyes boring into him.

'When you discovered the body, was it like this?'

'No,' said Montalbano, cool as a cucumber. 'She was naked.'

'And where did you get that bathrobe?'

'From the bathroom.'

'Put everything back as it was, for Christ's sake! You've altered the whole picture! That's very serious!'

Without a word, Montalbano walked over to the corpse, picked up the bathrobe, and draped it over his arm.

'Wow, nice arse!'

The comment came from one of the crime lab photographers, a homely sort of paparazzo with his shirt-tails hanging out of his trousers.

'Go right ahead, if you want,' the inspector said to him calmly. 'She's already in position.'

Fazio, who knew what dangers lurked beneath Montalbano's controlled calm, took a step towards him. The inspector looked Arquà in the eye, 'Understand now why I did it, arsehole?' And he left the room. In the bathroom he splashed a little water on his face, threw the bathrobe down on the floor more or less where he'd found it, and went back into the bedroom.

'I'll have to tell the commissioner about this,' Arquà said icily. Montalbano's voice was ten degrees icier.

'I'm sure you'll understand each other perfectly.'

＊

'Chief, me and Gallo and Galluzzo are going outside to smoke a cigarette. We're getting in these guys' way.'

Montalbano, absorbed in thought, didn't answer. From the living room he went back upstairs and examined the little guest room and the bathroom.

He'd already looked carefully around downstairs and hadn't found what he was looking for. For the sake of thoroughness, he stuck his head into the bedroom, which was being turned upside down by its invaders from the crime lab, and double-checked what he thought he'd seen earlier.

Outside the house, he lit a cigarette himself. Fazio had just finished talking on the mobile phone.

'I got the husband's phone number and address in Bologna,' he explained.

'Inspector,' Galluzzo broke in. 'We were just talking, the three of us. There's something strange—'

'The armoire in the bedroom is still wrapped in plastic,' Gallo cut in. 'And I also looked under the bed.'

'And I looked in all the other bedrooms. But—'

Fazio was about to draw the conclusion, but stopped when his superior raised a hand.

'The lady's clothes are nowhere to be found,' Montalbano concluded.

THREE

The ambulance arrived, followed by Coroner Pasquano's car.

'Go and see if forensics have finished with the bedroom,' Montalbano said to Galluzzo.

'Thanks,' said Dr Pasquano. His motto was: 'It's either me or them', 'them' being the forensics team. Jacomuzzi and his scruffy crew had been bad enough; how he put up with Dr Arquà and his visibly efficient staff, one could only imagine.

'A lot of work on your hands?' the inspector enquired.

'Not much. Five corpses this week. When have we ever seen that? Must be low season.'

Galluzzo returned to say that forensics had moved into the bathroom and guest room. The coast was clear.

'Accompany the doctor upstairs and come back down,' Montalbano said to Gallo. Pasquano shot him a glance of appreciation; he really liked to work alone.

After a good half hour, the judge's battered car

appeared and didn't stop until it had bumped into one of the crime lab's squad cars.

Nicolò Tommaseo got out, red in the face, his gallows-bird neck looking like a turkey cock's.

'What a dreadful road! I had two accidents!' he declared to one and all.

It was well known that he drove like a dog on drugs.

Montalbano found an excuse to prevent him from going upstairs at once and rattling Pasquano.

'Your Honour, let me tell you an extraordinary story.'

He told him part of what had happened to him the previous day. He pointed to the damage the Twingo had sustained from the impact, showed him the remnants of the scrap of paper he'd written on and slipped under the windscreen wiper, and explained how he'd begun to suspect something wasn't right. The anonymous phone call to the commissioner's office was the icing on the cake.

'What a curious coincidence!' Judge Tommaseo exclaimed, conceding no more than this.

As soon as the judge saw the victim's nude body, he froze. Even the inspector stopped dead in his tracks. Dr Pasquano had somehow managed to turn the woman's head, and now one could actually see her face, which had previously been buried in the bedclothes. The eyes were bulging to the point where they looked unreal, and they expressed unbearable pain and horror. A stream of blood trickled from her mouth. She must have bitten her tongue during the spasms of suffocation.

Dr Pasquano anticipated the question he hated so much.

'She definitely died sometime between late Wednesday night and early Thursday morning. I'll be able to say more precisely after the autopsy.'

'And how did she die?' asked Tommaseo.

'Can't you see? The killer pushed her face into the mattress and held her down until she was dead.'

'He must have been exceptionally strong.'

'Not necessarily.'

'Can you tell if they had relations before or after?'

'I can't say.'

Something in the judge's tone of voice led the inspector to look up at him. He was covered in sweat.

'He might have even sodomized her,' the judge went on, his eyes glistening.

It was a revelation. Apparently Justice Tommaseo secretly dipped into such subjects. Montalbano remembered having read somewhere a line by Manzoni about that more famous Nicolò Tommaseo, 'This Tommaseo with one foot in the sacristy and the other in the whorehouse.'

It must be a family vice.

'I'll let you know. Good day,' said Dr Pasquano, hastily taking leave to avoid any further questions.

'To my mind, it's the crime of a maniac who surprised the lady as she was going to bed,' Judge Tommaseo said firmly, without taking his eyes off the corpse.

'Look, Your Honour, there were no signs of a break-in. And it's rather unusual for a naked woman to open her front door to a maniac and take him up to her bedroom.'

'What kind of reasoning is that! She might not have noticed he was a maniac until ... You know what I mean?'

'I myself would lean towards a crime of passion,' said Montalbano, who was beginning to amuse himself.

'Indeed, why not? Why not?' said Tommaseo, jumping at the suggestion and scratching his beard. 'We must bear in mind that it was a woman who made the phone call. The betrayed wife. Speaking of which, do you know how to reach the victim's husband?'

'Yes, Sergeant Fazio has his telephone number,' the inspector replied, feeling his heart sink. He hated giving bad news.

'Let me have it. I'll take care of everything,' the judge said.

He had every kink in the book, this Nicolò Tommaseo. He was a raven to boot.

'Can we take her away now?' asked the ambulance crew, entering the room.

*

Another hour passed before the forensics team had finished fussing about and left.

'So now what do we do?' asked Gallo, who seemed to have become fixated on this question.

'Close the door, we're going back to Vigàta. I'm so hungry I can't see,' said the inspector.

*

Montalbano's housekeeper, Adelina, had left him a real delicacy in the fridge: 'coral' sauce, made of langoustine roe and sea-urchin pulp, to be used on spaghetti. He put the water on the stove and, while waiting, phoned his friend Nicolò Zito, newsman for the Free Channel, one of the two private television stations based in Montelusa. The other, TeleVigàta, whose news programming was anchored by Galluzzo's brother-in-law, tended to take a pro-government stance, regardless of who was running the country. Thus, given the government in power at that moment, and the fact that the Free Channel always leaned to the left, the two local stations might well be boringly similar if not for the lucid, ironic intelligence of the red-haired, red-sympathizing Nicolò Zito.

'Nicolò? Montalbano here. There's been a murder, but—'

'I'm not supposed to say it was you who told me about it.'

'An anonymous phone call. A female voice phoned the Montelusa commissioner's office this morning, saying a murder had been committed at a house in the Tre Fontane district. And it was true. A young woman, beautiful, naked—'

'Fuck.'

'Her name was Michela Licalzi.'

'Have you got a photo of her?'

'No, the murderer made off with her handbag and clothes.'

'Why did he do that?'

'I don't know.'

'So how do you know her name was Michela Licalzi? Has somebody identified her?'

'No. We're trying to contact her husband, who lives in Bologna.'

Nicolò asked him for a few more details, which he gave.

*

The water was boiling, so he put in the pasta. The telephone rang. He had a moment of hesitation, unsure whether to answer or not. He was afraid the call might last too long: it might not be so easy to cut it short, and that would jeopardize the proper al dente texture of the spaghetti. It would be a disaster to waste the coral sauce on a dish of overcooked pasta. He decided not to answer. In fact, to prevent the ringing from troubling the serenity of spirit indispensable to savouring the sauce in full, he pulled out the plug.

*

An hour later, pleased with himself and ready to meet the world head-on, he reconnected the telephone. He was forced to answer it at once.

'Hello.'

'Hullo, Chief? Izzatchoo y'self in poisson?'

'In poisson, Cat. What's up?'

'What's up is Judge Tolomeo called.'

'Tommaseo, Cat, but I get the picture. What did he want?'

'He wanted to speak poissonally wit' you y'self in poisson. He called at lease four times. Says you should call him y'self in poisson.'

'OK.'

'Oh, Chief, I got another streamly impoitant ting to tell ya. Somebody from Montelusa Central called to talk to me in poisson, Inspector Whatsizname, Tontona.'

'Tortona.'

'Whatever's 'is name. Him. Says I gotta take a concourse in pewters. Whattya think, boss?'

'I'm happy for you, Cat. Take the course, you can become a specialist. You're just the right man for pewters.'

'Thanks, Chief.'

✻

'Hello, Judge Tommaseo? Montalbano here.'

'Inspector, I've been looking all over for you.'

'Forgive me, I was very busy. Remember the investigation into the body that was found in the water last week? I think you were duly informed about it.'

'Any new developments?'

'No, none whatsoever.'

Montalbano sensed the judge's silent confusion. The exchange they'd just had was entirely meaningless. As he'd expected, the judge didn't linger on the subject.

'I wanted to tell you I tracked down the widower, Dr Licalzi, in Bologna, and, tactfully, of course, gave him the terrible news.'

'How did he react?'

'Well, how shall I put it? Strangely. He didn't even ask what his wife died of. She was very young, after all. He must be a cold one; he hardly got upset at all.'

Dr Licalzi had denied the raven Tommaseo his jollies. The judge's disappointment at not having been able to relish a fine display of cries and sobs – however long distance – was palpable.

'At any rate he said he absolutely could not absent himself from the hospital today. He had some operations to perform and his replacement was sick. He's going to take the 7.05 flight for Palermo tomorrow morning. I assume, therefore, he'll be at your office around midday. I just wanted to bring you up to date on this.'

'Thank you, sir.'

*

As Gallo was driving the inspector to work in a squad car, he informed Montalbano that, on Fazio's orders, patrolman Germanà had picked up the damaged Twingo and put it in the police station's garage.

'Good idea.'

The first person to enter his office was Mimì Augello.

'I'm not here to talk to you about work. The day after tomorrow, that is, early Sunday morning, I'm going to visit my sister. D'you want to come, too, so you can see François? We'll drive back in the evening.'

'I'll do my best to make it.'

'Try to come. My sister made it clear she wants to talk to you.'

'About François?'

'Yes.'

Montalbano became anxious. He'd be in quite a fix if Augello's sister and her husband said they couldn't keep the kid with them any longer.

'I'll do what I can, Mimì. Thanks.'

*

'Hello, Inspector Montalbano? This is Clementina Vasile Cozzo.'

'What a pleasure, signora.'

'Answer me yes or no. Was I good?'

'You were great, yes.'

'Answer me yes or no again. Are you coming to dinner tonight at nine?'

'Yes.'

*

Fazio walked into his office with a triumphant air.

'Know what, Chief? I asked myself a question: with

the house looking the way it did, like it was only occasionally lived in, where did Mrs Licalzi sleep when she came here from Bologna? So I called a colleague at Montelusa Central Police, the guy assigned to the hotel beat, and I got my answer. Every time she came, Michela Licalzi stayed at the Hotel Jolly in Montelusa. Turns out she last checked in seven days ago.'

Fazio caught him off balance. He'd intended to call Dr Licalzi in Bologna as soon as he got into work, but had been distracted. Mimi's mention of François had flustered him a little.

'Shall we go there now?' asked Fazio.

'Wait.'

An idea had flashed into his brain utterly unprovoked, leaving behind an ever-so-slight scent of sulphur, the kind the devil usually likes to wear. He asked Fazio for Licalzi's telephone number, wrote it down on a piece of paper which he put in his pocket, then dialled it.

'Hello, Central Hospital? Inspector Montalbano here, from Vigàta police, in Sicily. I'd like to speak to Dr Emanuele Licalzi.'

'Please hold.'

He waited, all patience and self-control. When he appeared to be running out of both, the operator came back on the line.

'Dr Licalzi is in the operating theatre. You'll have to try again in half an hour.'

'I'll call him from the car,' he said to Fazio. 'Bring along your mobile phone, don't forget.'

He rang Judge Tommaseo and informed him of Fazio's discovery.

'Oh, I forgot to tell you,' Tommaseo interjected. 'When I asked him to give me his wife's number here, he said he didn't know it. He said it was always she who called him.'

The inspector asked the judge to prepare him a search warrant. He would send Gallo over at once to pick it up.

'Fazio, did they tell you what Dr Licalzi's speciality is?'

'Yes, he's an orthopedic surgeon.'

*

Halfway between Vigàta and Montelusa, the inspector called Bologna Central Hospital again. After not too long a wait, Montalbano heard a firm, polite voice.

'This is Licalzi. With whom am I speaking?'

'Excuse me for disturbing you, Doctor. I'm Inspector Salvo Montalbano of the Vigàta police. I'm handling the case. Please allow me to express my sincerest condolences.'

'Thank you.'

Not one word more or less. The inspector realized it was still up to him to talk.

'Well, Doctor, you told the judge today that you didn't know your wife's phone number here in Vigàta.'

'That's correct.'

'We've been unable to track down this number ourselves.'

'There could hardly be thousands of hotels in Monte-lusa and Vigàta.'

Ready to cooperate, this Dr Licalzi.

'Forgive me for insisting. But hadn't you arranged, in case of dire need—'

'I don't think such a need could have ever arisen. In any case, there's a distant relative of mine who lives in Vigàta and with whom my poor Michela had been in contact.'

'Could you tell me—'

'His name is Aurelio Di Blasi. And now you must excuse me, I have to return to the operating theatre. I'll be at your office tomorrow, around midday.'

'One last question. Have you told this relative what happened?'

'No. Why? Should I have?'

FOUR

'Such an exquisite, elegant lady, and so beautiful!' said Claudio Pizzotta, the distinguished, sixtyish manager of the Hotel Jolly in Montelusa. 'Has something happened to her?'

'We don't really know yet. We got a phone call from her husband in Bologna, who was worried.'

'Right. As far as I know, Signora Licalzi left the hotel on Wednesday evening, and we haven't seen her since.'

'Weren't you worried? It's already Friday evening, if I'm not mistaken.'

'Right.'

'Did she let you know she wouldn't be returning?'

'No. But, you see, Inspector, the lady has been staying with us regularly for at least two years, so we've had a lot of time to become acquainted with her habits. Which are, well, unusual. Signora Michela is not the sort of woman to go unnoticed, you know what I mean? And then, I've always had my own worries about her.'

'You have? And what would they be?'

'Well, the lady owns a lot of valuable jewellery. Necklaces, bracelets, earrings, rings ... I've asked her many times to deposit them in our safe, but she always refuses. She keeps them in a kind of bag; she doesn't carry a handbag. She always tells me not to worry, says she doesn't leave the jewels in her room, but carries them around with her. I've also been afraid she'll get robbed on the street. But she always smiles and says no. She just won't be persuaded.'

'You mentioned her unusual habits. Could you be more precise?'

'Certainly. The lady likes to stay up late. She often comes home at the first light of dawn.'

'Alone?'

'Always.'

'Drunk? High?'

'Never. Or at least, so says the night porter.'

'Mind telling me why you were talking about Mrs Licalzi with the night porter?'

Claudio Pizzotta turned bright red. Apparently he'd had ideas about dunking his doughnut with Signora Michela.

'Inspector, surely you understand ... A beautiful woman like that, alone ... One's curiosity is bound to be aroused, it's only natural.'

'Go on. Tell me about her habits.'

'The lady sleeps in till about midday, and doesn't want to be disturbed in any way. When she wakes up, she orders breakfast in her room and starts making and receiving phone calls.'

'A lot of phone calls?'

'I've got an itemized list that never ends.'

'Do you know who she was calling?'

'One could find out. But it's a bit complicated. From your room you need only dial zero and you can phone New Zealand if you want.'

'What about the incoming calls?'

'Well, there's not much to say about that. The switchboard operator takes the call and passes it on to the room. There's only one way to know.'

'And that is?'

'When somebody calls and leaves his name when the client is out. In that case, the porter is given a message that he puts in the client's key box.'

'Does the lady lunch at the hotel?'

'Rarely. After eating a hearty breakfast so late, you can imagine ... But it has happened. Actually, the head waiter once told me how self-possessed she is at table when eating lunch.'

'I'm sorry, I don't follow.'

'Our hotel is very popular, with businessmen, politicians, entrepreneurs. In one way or another, they all end up trying their luck. A beckoning glance, a smile, more or less explicit invitations. The amazing thing about Signora Michela, the head waiter said, is that she never plays the prude, never takes offence, but actually returns the glances

and smiles. But when it comes to the nitty-gritty, nothing
doing. They're left high and dry.'

'And at what time in the afternoon does she usually go
out?'

'About four. Then returns in the dead of night.'

'She must have a pretty broad circle of friends in
Montelusa and Vigàta.'

'I'd say so.'

'Has she ever stayed out for more than one night
before?'

'I don't think so. The porter would have told me.'

Gallo and Galluzzo arrived, flourishing the search
warrant.

'What room is Mrs Licalzi staying in?'

'Number one-eighteen.'

'I've got a warrant.'

The hotel manager looked offended.

'Inspector! There was no need for that formality! You
had only to ask and I ... Let me show you the way.'

'No, thanks,' Montalbano said curtly.

The manager's face went from looking offended to
looking mortally offended.

'I'll go and get the key,' he said aloofly.

He returned a moment later with the key and a little
stack of papers, all notes of incoming phone calls.

'Here,' he said, giving, for no apparent reason, the key
to Fazio and the message slips to Gallo. Then he bowed
his head abruptly, German-style, in front of Montalbano,

turned around and walked stiffly away, looking like a wooden puppet in motion.

*

Room 118 was eternally imbued with the scent of Chanel No. 5. On the luggage rack sat two suitcases and a shoulder bag, all Louis Vuitton. Montalbano opened the armoire: five very classy dresses, three pairs of artfully worn-out jeans; in the shoe section, five pairs of Bruno Maglis with spike heels and three pairs of casual flats. The blouses, also very costly, were folded with extreme care; the underwear, divided by colour in its assigned drawer, consisted only of airy panties.

'Nothing in here,' said Fazio, who in the meantime had examined the two suitcases and shoulder bag.

Gallo and Galluzzo, who had upended the bed and mattress, shook their heads no and began putting everything back in place, impressed by the order that reigned in the room.

On the small desk were some letters, notes, a diary, and a stack of telephone messages considerably taller than the one the manager had given to Gallo.

'We'll take these things away with us,' the inspector said to Fazio. 'Look in the drawers, too. Take all the papers.'

From his pocket Fazio withdrew a plastic bag that he always carried with him, and began to fill it.

Montalbano went into the bathroom. Sparkling clean,

in perfect order. On the shelf, Rouge Idole lipstick, Shiseido foundation, a magnum of Chanel No. 5, and so on. A pink bathrobe, obviously softer and more expensive than the one in the house, hung placidly on a hook.

He went back into the bedroom and rang for the floor attendant. A moment later there was a knock and Montalbano told her to come in. The door opened and a gaunt, fortyish woman appeared. As soon as she saw the four men, she stiffened, blanched, and in a faint voice said, 'Are you police?'

The inspector laughed. How many centuries of police tyranny had it taken to hone this Sicilian woman's ability to detect law-enforcement officers at a moment's glance?

'Yes, we are,' he said, smiling.

The chambermaid blushed and lowered her eyes.

'Please excuse me.'

'Do you know Mrs Licalzi?'

'Why, what's happened to her?'

'She hasn't been heard from for a couple of days. We're looking for her.'

'And to look for her you have to take all her papers away?'

This woman was not to be underestimated. Montalbano decided to admit a few things to her.

'We're afraid something bad may have happened to her.'

'I always told her to be careful,' said the maid. 'She goes around with half a billion in her bag!'

'She went around with that much money?' Montalbano asked in astonishment.

'I wasn't talking about money, but the jewels she owns. And with the kind of life she leads! Comes home late, gets up late . . .'

'We already know that. Do you know her well?'

'Sure. Since she came here the first time with her husband.'

'Can you tell me anything about what she's like?'

'Look, she never made any trouble. She was just a maniac for order. Whenever we did her room, she would stand there making sure that everything was put back in its place. The girls on the morning shift always ask for the good Lord's help before working on one-eighteen.'

'A final question: did your colleagues on the morning shift ever mention if the lady'd had men in her room at night?'

'Never. And we've got an eye for that kind of thing.'

*

The whole way back to Vigàta one question tormented Montalbano: if the lady was a maniac for order, why was the bathroom at the house in Tre Fontane such a mess, with the pink bathrobe thrown haphazardly on the floor to boot?

*

During the dinner (super-fresh cod poached with a couple of bay leaves and dressed directly on the plate with salt, pepper and Pantelleria olive oil, with a side dish of gentle *tinnirùme* to cheer the stomach and intestines), the inspector told Mrs Vasile Cozzo of the day's developments.

'As far as I can tell,' said Clementina, 'the real question is: why did the murderer make off with the poor woman's clothes, underwear, shoes and handbag?'

'Yes,' Montalbano commented, saying nothing more. She'd hit the nail on the head as soon as she opened her mouth, and he didn't want to interrupt her thought processes.

'But I can only talk about these things,' the elderly woman continued, 'based on what I see on television.'

'Don't you read mystery novels?'

'Not very often. Anyway, what does that mean, "mystery novel"? What *is* a "detective novel"?'

'Well, it's a whole body of literature that—'

'Of course, but I don't like labels. Want me to tell you a good mystery story? All right, there's a man who, after many adventures, becomes the leader of a city. Little by little, however, his subjects begin to fall ill with an unknown sickness, a kind of plague. And so this man sets about to discover the cause of the illness, and in the course of his investigations he discovers that he himself is the root of it all. And so he punishes himself.'

'Oedipus,' Montalbano said, as if to himself.

'Now isn't that a good detective story? But, to return

to our discussion: why would a killer make off with the victim's clothes? The first answer is: so she couldn't be identified.'

'That's not the case here,' the inspector said.

'Right. And I get the feeling that, by reasoning this way, we're following the path the killer wants us to take.'

'I don't understand.'

'What I mean is, whoever made off with all those things wants us to believe that every one of them is of equal importance to him. He wants us to think of that stuff as a single whole. Whereas that is not the case.'

'Yes,' Montalbano said again, ever more impressed, and ever more reluctant to break the thread of her argument with some untimely observation.

'For one thing, the handbag alone is worth half a billion because of the jewellery inside it. To a common thief, robbing the bag would itself constitute a good day's earnings. Right?'

'Right.'

'But what reason would a common thief have for taking her clothes? None whatsoever. Therefore, if he made off with her clothes, underwear and shoes, we should conclude that we're not dealing with a common thief. But, in fact, he *is* a common thief who has done this only to make us think he's uncommon, different. Why? He might have done it to shuffle the cards. He wanted to steal the handbag with all its valuables, but since he committed murder, he wanted to mask his real purpose.'

'Right,' said Montalbano, unsolicited.

'To continue. Maybe the thief made off with other things of value that we're unaware of.'

'May I make a phone call?' asked the inspector, who had suddenly had an idea.

He called up the Hotel Jolly in Montelusa and asked to speak with Claudio Pizzotta, the manager.

'Oh, Inspector, how atrocious! How terrible! We found out just now from the Free Channel that poor Mrs Licalzi...'

Nicolò Zito had reported the news and Montalbano had forgotten to tune in and see how the newsman presented the story.

'TeleVigàta also did a report,' added the hotel manager, torn between genuine satisfaction and feigned grief.

Galluzzo had done his job with his brother-in-law.

'What should I do, Inspector?' the manager asked, distressed.

'What do you mean?'

'About these journalists. They're besieging me. They want to interview me. They found out the poor woman was staying with us...'

From whom could they have learned this if not from the manager himself? The inspector imagined Pizzotta on the phone, summoning reporters with the promise of shocking revelations on the young, attractive, and, most importantly, naked murder victim...

'Do whatever the hell you want. Listen, did Mrs Licalzi normally wear any of the jewellery she had? Did she own a watch?'

'Of course she wore it. Discreetly, though. Otherwise, why would she bring it all here from Bologna? As for the watch, she always wore a splendid, paper-thin Piaget on her wrist.'

Montalbano thanked him, hung up, and told Signora Clementina what he'd just learned. She thought about it a minute.

'We must now establish whether we are dealing with a thief who became a murderer out of necessity, or with a murderer who is pretending to be a thief.'

'For no real reason – by instinct, I guess – I don't believe in this thief.'

'You're wrong to trust your instinct.'

'But, Signora Clementina, Michela Licalzi was naked, she'd just finished taking a shower. A thief would have heard the noise and waited before coming inside.'

'And what makes you think the thief wasn't already inside when the lady came home? She comes in, and the burglar hides. When she goes into the shower, he decides the time is right. He comes out of his hiding place, steals whatever he's supposed to steal, but then she catches him in the act, and he reacts in the manner he does. He may not even have intended to kill her.'

'But how would this burglar have entered?'

'The same way you did, Inspector.'

A direct hit, and down he went. Montalbano said nothing.

'Now for the clothes,' Signora Clementina continued. 'If they were stolen just for show, that's one thing. But if the murderer needed to get rid of them, that's another kettle of fish. What could have been so important about them?'

'They might have represented a danger to him, a way of identifying him,' said Montalbano.

'Yes, you're right, Inspector. But they clearly weren't a danger when the woman put them on. They must have become so afterwards. How?'

'Maybe they got stained,' Montalbano said, unconvinced. 'Maybe even with the killer's blood. Even though . . .'

'Even though?'

'Even though there was no blood around the bedroom. There was a little on the sheet, which had come out of Mrs Licalzi's mouth. But maybe it was another kind of stain. Like vomit, for example.'

'Or semen,' said Mrs Vasile Cozzo, blushing.

*

It was too early to go home to Marinella, so Montalbano decided to put in an appearance at the station to see if there were any new developments.

'Oh, Chief, Chief!' said Catarella as soon as he saw him. 'You're here? At least ten people called, and they all wanted a talk to you in poisson! I didn't know you was comin' so I says to all of 'em to call back tomorrow morning. Did I do right, Chief?'

'You did right, Cat, don't worry about it. Do you know what they wanted?'

'They all said as how they all knew the lady who was murdered.'

On the desk in his office, Fazio had left the plastic bag with the papers they'd seized from room 118. Next to it were the notices of incoming calls that the manager Pizzotta had turned over to Gallo. The inspector sat down, took the diary out of the bag, and glanced through it. Michela Licalzi's diary was as orderly as her hotel room: appointments, telephone calls to make, places to go. Everything was carefully and clearly written down.

Dr Pasquano had said the woman was killed sometime between late Wednesday night and early Thursday morning, and Montalbano agreed with this. He looked up the page for Wednesday, the last day of Michela Licalzi's life – 4 p.m., Rotondo's Furniture; 4.30 p.m., phone Emanuele; 5 p.m., appt with Todaro gardeners; 6 p.m., Anna; 8 p.m., dinner with the Vassallos.

The woman, however, had made other engagements for Thursday, Friday and Saturday, unaware that someone would prevent her from attending them. On Thursday, again in the afternoon, she was to have met with Anna, with whom she was to go to Loconte's (in parentheses: 'curtains') before ending her evening by dining with a

certain Maurizio. On Friday she was supposed to see
Riguccio the electrician, meet Anna again, then go out to
dinner at the Cangelosi home. On the page for Saturday,
all that was written down was: '4.30 p.m., flight from
Punta Ràisi to Bologna.'

It was a large-format diary. The telephone index
allowed three pages for each letter of the alphabet, but
she'd copied down so many phone numbers that in certain
cases she'd had to write the numbers of two different
people on the same line.

Montalbano set the diary aside and took the other
papers out of the bag. Nothing of interest. Just invoices
and receipts. Every penny spent on the construction and
furnishing of the house was fastidiously accounted for.
In a square-lined notebook Michela had copied down
every expense in neat columns, as if preparing herself
for a visit from the revenue officers. There was a cheque
book from the Banca Popolare di Bologna with only the
stubs remaining. Montalbano also found a boarding pass
for Bologna–Rome–Palermo from six days earlier, and
a return ticket, Palermo–Rome–Bologna, for Saturday at
4.30 p.m.

No sign whatsoever of any personal letter or note. He
decided to continue working at home.

FIVE

The only things left to examine were the notices of incoming calls. The inspector began with the ones Michela had collected in the little desk in her hotel room. There were about forty of them, and Montalbano arranged them according to the name of the person calling. In the end he was left with three small piles somewhat taller than the rest. A woman, Anna, would call during the day and usually leave word that Michela should call her back as soon as she woke up or when she got back in. A man, Maurizio, had rung two or three times in the morning, but normally preferred the late-night hours and always insisted that she call him back. The third caller was also male, Guido by name, and he phoned from Bologna, also late at night; but, unlike Maurizio, he never left a message.

The slips of paper the hotel manager had given to Gallo were twenty in number: all from the time Michela left the hotel on Wednesday afternoon to the moment the police showed up at the hotel. On Wednesday morning, however, during the hours Mrs Licalzi devoted to sleep, the same Maurizio had asked for her at about ten thirty, and Anna had done likewise shortly thereafter. Around nine o'clock that evening, Mrs Vassallo had called looking for Michela, and had rung back an hour later. Anna had phoned back shortly before midnight.

At three o'clock on Thursday morning, Guido had called from Bologna. At ten thirty, Anna, apparently unaware that Michela hadn't returned to the hotel that night, called again; at eleven, a certain Mr Loconte called to confirm the afternoon appointment. At midday, still on Thursday, a Mr Aurelio Di Blasi phoned and continued to phone back almost every three hours until early Friday evening. Guido from Bologna had called at two o'clock on Friday morning. As of Thursday morning, Anna had started calling frantically and also didn't stop until Friday evening.

Something didn't add up. Montalbano couldn't put his finger on it, and this made him uncomfortable. He stood up, went out on the veranda, which gave directly onto the beach, took off his shoes, and started walking in the sand until he reached the water's edge. He rolled up his trouser legs and began wading in the water, which from time to time washed over his feet. The soothing sound of the waves helped him put his thoughts in order. Suddenly he understood what was tormenting him. He went back in the house, grabbed the diary, and opened it up to Wednesday. Michela had written down that she was supposed to go to dinner at the Vassallos' house at eight. So why had Mrs Vassallo called her at the hotel at nine and again at ten? Hadn't Michela shown up for dinner? Or did the Mrs Vassallo who phoned have nothing to do with the Vassallos who'd invited her to dinner?

He glanced at his watch: past midnight. He decided the matter was too important to be worrying about etiquette. There turned out to be three listings under Vassallo in the phone book. He tried the first and guessed right.

'I'm very sorry. This is Inspector Montalbano.'

'Inspector! I'm Ernesto Vassallo. I was going to come to your office myself tomorrow morning. My wife is just devastated; I had to call a doctor. Is there any news?'

'None. I need to ask you something.'

'Go right ahead, Inspector. For poor Michela—'

Montalbano cut him off.

'I read in Mrs Licalzi's diary that she was supposed to have dinner—'

This time it was Ernesto Vassallo who interrupted.

'She never showed up, Inspector! We waited a long time for her. But nothing, not even a phone call. And she was always so punctual! We got worried, we thought she might be sick, so we rang the hotel a couple of times, then we tried her friend Anna Tropeano, but she said she didn't know anything. She said she'd seen Michela at about six and they'd been together for roughly half an hour, and that Michela had left saying she was going back to the hotel to change before coming to dinner at our place.'

'Listen, I really appreciate your help. But don't come to the station tomorrow morning, I'm full up with appointments. Drop by in the afternoon whenever you want. Goodnight.'

One good turn deserved another. He looked up the number for Aurelio Di Blasi in the phone book and dialled it. The first ring wasn't even over when someone picked up.

'Hello? Hello? Is that you?'

The voice of a middle-aged man, breathless, troubled.

'Inspector Montalbano here.'

'Oh.'

Montalbano could tell that the man felt profound disappointment. From whom was he so anxiously awaiting a phone call?

'Mr Di Blasi, I'm sure you've heard about the unfortunate Mrs—'

'I know, I know, I saw it on TV.'

The disappointment had been replaced by undisguised irritation.

'Anyway, I wanted to know why, from midday on Thursday to Friday evening, you repeatedly tried to reach Mrs Licalzi at her hotel.'

'What's so unusual about that? I'm a distant relative of Michela's. Whenever she came to Vigàta to work on the house, she would lean on me for help and advice. I'm a construction engineer. I phoned her on Thursday to invite her here to dinner, but the receptionist said she hadn't come back that night. The receptionist knows me, we're friends. And so I started to get worried. Is that so hard to understand?'

Now Mr Di Blasi had turned sarcastic and aggressive. The inspector had the impression the man's nerves were about to pop.

'No.'

There was no point in calling Anna Tropeano. He already knew what she would say, since Mr Vassallo had told him beforehand. He would summon Ms Tropeano to the station for questioning. One thing at this point was certain: Michela Licalzi had disappeared from circulation at approximately seven o'clock on Wednesday evening. She had never returned to the hotel, even though she'd expressed this intention to her friend.

He wasn't sleepy, so he lay down in bed with a book, a novel by Marco Denevi, an Argentine writer he liked very much.

*

When his eyes started to droop, he closed the book and turned off the light. As he often did before falling asleep, he thought of Livia. Suddenly he sat up in bed, wide awake. Jesus, Livia! He hadn't phoned her back since the night of the storm, when he'd made it seem as if the line had been cut. Livia clearly hadn't believed this, since in fact she'd never phoned back. He had to set things right at once.

'Hello? Who is this?' said Livia's sleepy voice.

'It's Salvo, darling.'

'Oh, let me sleep, for Christ's sake!'

Click. Montalbano sat there for a while holding the receiver.

*

It was eight thirty in the morning when Montalbano walked into the station carrying Michela Licalzi's papers. After Livia had refused to speak to him, he'd become agitated and unable to sleep a wink. There was no need to call in Anna Tropeano; Fazio immediately told him the woman had been waiting for him since eight.

'Listen, I want to know everything there is to know about a construction engineer from Vigàta named Aurelio Di Blasi.'

'Everything everything?' asked Fazio.

'Everything everything.'

'To me, everything everything means rumours and gossip, too.'

'Same here.'

'How much time do I get?'

'Come on, Fazio, you playing the unionist now? Two hours ought to be more than enough.'

Fazio glared at his boss with an air of indignation and went out without even saying goodbye.

*

In normal circumstances, Anna Tropeano must have been an attractive woman of thirty, with jet-black hair, dark complexion, big, sparkling eyes, tall and full-bodied. On this occasion, however, her shoulders were hunched, her eyes swollen and red, her skin turning a shade of grey.

'May I smoke?' she asked, sitting down.

'Of course.'

She lit a cigarette, hands trembling. She attempted a rough imitation of a smile.

'I quit only a week ago. But since last night I must have smoked at least three packets.'

'Thanks for coming in on your own. I really need a lot of information from you.'

'That's what I'm here for.'

Montalbano secretly breathed a sigh of relief. Anna was a strong woman. There wasn't going to be any sobbing or fainting. In fact, she had appealed to him from the moment he saw her in the doorway.

'Even if some of my questions seem odd to you, please try to answer them anyway.'

'Of course.'

'Married?'

'Who?'

'You.'

'No, I'm not. Not separated or divorced, either. And not even engaged. Nothing. I live alone.'

'Why?'

Though Montalbano had forewarned her, Anna hesitated a moment before answering so personal a question.

'I don't think I've had time to think about myself, Inspector. A year before graduating from university, my father died. Heart attack. He was very young. The year after I graduated, my mother died. I had to look after my little sister, Maria, who's nineteen now and married and living in Milan, and my brother, Giuseppe, who works at a bank in Rome and is twenty-seven. I'm thirty-one. But aside from all that, I don't think I've ever met the right person.'

There was no resentment. On the contrary, she seemed slightly calmer now. The fact that the inspector hadn't launched immediately into the matter at hand had allowed her in a sense to catch her breath. Montalbano thought it best to steer clear for a while.

'Do you live in your parents' house here in Vigàta?'

'Yes, Papa bought it. It's sort of a small villa, right where Marinella begins. It's become too big for me.'

'The one on the right, just after the bridge?'

'That's the one.'

'I pass by it at least twice a day. I live in Marinella myself.'

Anna Tropeano eyed him with mild amazement. What a strange sort of policeman!

'Do you work?'

'Yes, I teach at the *liceo scientifico* of Montelusa.'

'What do you teach?'

'Physics.'

Montalbano looked at her with admiration. In physics, at school, he'd always been between a D and an F. If he'd had a teacher like her in his day, he might have become another Einstein.

'Do you know who killed her?'

Anna Tropeano jumped in her chair and looked at him imploringly: we were getting along so well, why do you want to play policeman, which is worse than playing hunting dog?

Don't you ever let go? she seemed to be asking.

Montalbano, who understood what the woman's eyes were saying to him, smiled and threw up his hands in a gesture of resignation, as if to say: *It's my job.*

'No,' replied a firm, decisive Anna Tropeano.

'Any suspicion?'

'No.'

'Mrs Licalzi customarily returned to her hotel in the wee hours of the morning. I'd like to know—'

'She was at my house. We had dinner together almost every night. And if she was invited out, she would come along afterwards.'

'What did you do together?'

'What do two women friends usually do when they see each other? We talked, we watched television, we listened to music. Sometimes we did nothing at all. It was a pleasure just to know the other one was there.'

'Did she have any male friends?'

'Yes, a few. But things were not what they seemed. Michela was a very serious person. Seeing her so free and easy, men got the wrong impression. And they were always disappointed, without fail.'

'Was there anyone in particular who bothered her a lot?'

'Yes.'

'What's his name?'

'I'm not going to tell you. You'll find out soon enough.'

'So, in short, Mrs Licalzi was faithful to her husband.'

'I didn't say that.'

'What does that mean?'

'It means what I said.'

'Had you known each other a long time?'

'No.'

Montalbano looked at her, stood up, and walked over to the window. Anna, almost angrily, lit up another cigarette.

'I don't like the tone you've assumed in the last part of our dialogue,' the inspector said with his back to her.

'I don't either.'

'Peace?'

'Peace.'

Montalbano turned around and smiled at her. Anna smiled back. But only for an instant. Then she raised a finger like a schoolgirl, wanting to ask a question.

'Can you tell me, if it's not a secret, how she was killed?'

'They didn't say so on TV?'

'No. Neither the Free Channel nor TeleVigàta said anything. They only said the body had been found.'

'I shouldn't be telling you. But I'll make an exception. She was suffocated.'

'With a pillow?'

'No, with her face pressed down against the mattress.'

Anna began to sway, the way treetops sway in strong wind. The inspector left the room and returned a moment later with a bottle of water and a glass. Anna drank as if she had just come out of the desert.

'But what was she doing there at the house, for God's sake?' she asked, as if to herself.

'Have you ever been to that house?'

'Of course. Almost daily, with her.'

'Did she ever sleep there?'

'No, not that I know of.'

'But there was a bathrobe in the bathroom, and towels and creams—'

'I know. Michela put those things there on purpose. Whenever she went to work on the house, she ended up all covered in dust and cement. So, before leaving, she would take a shower.'

Montalbano decided it was time to hit below the belt. But he felt reluctant; he didn't want to injure her too badly.

'She was completely naked.'

Anna looked as if a high-voltage charge had passed through her. Eyes popping out of her head, she tried to say something but couldn't. Montalbano refilled her glass.

'Was she . . . was she raped?'

'I don't know. The pathologist hasn't told me yet.'

'But why didn't she go back to her hotel instead of going to that goddamned house?' Anna asked herself again in despair.

'Whoever killed her also took all her clothes, under-wear and shoes.'

Anna looked at him in disbelief, as though the inspector had just told her a big lie.

'For what reason?'

Montalbano didn't answer. He continued, 'He even made off with her handbag and everything that was in it.'

'That's a little more understandable. Michela used to keep all her jewellery in it, and she had a lot, all very valuable. If the person who suffocated her was a thief—'

'Wait. Mr Vassallo told me that when Michela didn't show up to dinner at his place, they got worried and phoned you.'

'That's true. I thought she was at their house. When

Michela left me, she'd said she was stopping off at the hotel to change her clothes.'

'Speaking of which, how was she dressed?'

'Entirely in denim – jeans and jacket – and casual shoes.'

'She never went back to the hotel. Somebody or something made her change her mind. Did she have a mobile phone?'

'Yes, she kept it in her bag.'

'So it's possible that someone phoned Mrs Licalzi as she was going back to the hotel. And that as a result of this phone call, she went out to the house.'

'Maybe it was a trap.'

'Set by whom? Certainly not by a thief. Have you ever heard of a burglar summoning the owner of the house he's about to rob?'

'Did you notice if anything was missing from the house?'

'Her Piaget, for certain. As for everything else, I'm not sure. I don't know what things of value she had in the house. Everything looked to be in order, except for the bathroom, which was a mess.'

'A mess?'

'Yes. The pink bathrobe was thrown on the floor. She'd just finished taking a shower.'

'Inspector, I find the picture you're presenting totally unconvincing.'

'What do you mean?'

'I mean, the idea that Michela would go to the house to meet a man and be in such a rush to go to bed with him that she would throw off her bathrobe and let it fall wherever it happened to fall.'

'That's plausible, isn't it?'

'Maybe for other women, but not Michela.'

'Do you know somebody named Guido who called her every night from Bologna?'

He'd fired blindly, but hit the mark. Anna Tropeano looked away, embarrassed.

'You said a few minutes ago that Mrs Licalzi was faithful,' he continued.

'Yes.'

'Faithful to her one infidelity?'

Anna nodded yes.

'Could you tell me his name? You see, you'll be doing me a favour. It'll save me time. Because, don't worry, I'll find out eventually anyway. Well?'

'His name is Guido Serravalle. He's an antique dealer. I don't know his telephone number or address.'

'Thanks, that's good enough. Her husband will be here around midday. Would you like to see him?'

'Me? Why? I don't even know him.'

The inspector didn't need to ask any more questions. Anna went on talking of her own accord.

'Michela married Dr Licalzi two and a half years ago. It was her idea to come to Sicily for their honeymoon. But that's not when we met. That happened later, when she returned by herself with the intention of having a house built. I was on my way to Montelusa one day and a Twingo was coming from the opposite direction, we were both distracted, and we narrowly avoided a head-on collision. We both pulled over and got out to apologize, and took an immediate liking to each other. Every time Michela came down after that, she always came alone.'

She was tired. Montalbano took pity on her.

'You've been very helpful to me. Thank you.'

'Can I go?'

'Of course.'

He extended his hand to her. Anna Tropeano took it and held it between both of hers.

The inspector felt a wave of heat rise up inside him.

'Thank you,' said Anna.

'For what?'

'For letting me talk about Michela. I don't have anybody to ... Thanks. I feel calmer now.'

SIX

No sooner had Anna Tropeano left than the door to the inspector's office flew open, slamming into the wall, and Catarella came barrelling into the room.

'The next time you come in here like that, I'm going to shoot you. And you know I mean it,' Montalbano said calmly.

Catarella, however, was too excited to worry about this.

'Chief, I just wanna say I got a call from the c'missioner's office. Remember the concourse in pewters I tol' you 'bout? Well, it starts Monday morning an' I gotta be there. Whatcha gonna do witout me onna phone?'

'We'll survive, Cat.'

'Oh, Chief, Chief! You said you dint wanna be distroubled when you was talking wit da lady an' I did what you said! But inna meantime you gotta lotta phone calls! I wrote 'em all down on dis li'l piece a paper.'

'Give it to me and get out of here.'

On a poorly torn-out piece of notebook paper was

written, 'Phone calls: Vizzallo Guito Sarah Valli Losconti yer frend Zito Rotonò Totano Ficuccio Cangialosi Sarah Valli of Bolonia agin Cipollina Pinissi Cacamo.'

Montalbano started scratching himself all over. It must have been some mysterious form of allergy, but every time he was forced to read something Catarella had written, an irresistible itch came over him. With the patience of a saint, he deciphered: Vassallo, Guido Serravalle (Michela's Bolognese lover), Loconte (who sold fabric for curtains), his friend Nicolò Zito, Rotondo (the furniture salesman), Todaro (the plant and garden man), Riguccio (the electrician), Cangelosi (who'd invited Michela to dinner) and Serravalle again. Cipollina, Pinissi and Cacamo, assuming that those were their real names, were unfamiliar to him, but in all likelihood they had phoned because they were friends or acquaintances of the murder victim.

'May I?' asked Fazio, sticking his head inside the door.

'Come on in. Did you get the low-down on the engineer Di Blasi?'

'Of course. Why else would I be here?'

Fazio was apparently expecting to be praised for having taken such a short time to gather the information.

'See? You did it in less than an hour,' the inspector said instead.

Fazio darkened.

'Is that the kind of thanks I get?'

'Why do you want to be thanked just for doing your duty?'

'Inspector, may I say something, with all due respect? This morning you're downright obnoxious.'

'By the way, why haven't I yet had the honour and pleasure, so to speak, of seeing Inspector Augello at the office this morning?'

'He's out today with Germanà and Galluzzo looking into that business at the cement works.'

'What's this about?'

'You don't know? Yesterday, about thirty-five workers at the cement factory were given pink slips. This morning they started raising hell, shouting, throwing stones. The manager got scared and called us up.'

'And why did Mimì Augello go?'

'The manager asked him for help!'

'Jesus Christ! If I've said it once, I've said it a thousand times. I don't want anyone from my station getting mixed up in these things!'

'But what was Augello supposed to do?'

'He should have passed the phone call on to the carabinieri, who get off on that kind of thing! Mr Manager's always going to find another position when the going gets tough. The ones who get thrown out on their arses are the workers. And we're supposed to club them over the head?'

'Chief, excuse me again, but you're really and truly a communist, a hotheaded communist.'

'Fazio, you're stuck on this communist crap. I'm not a

communist, will you get that in your head once and for all?'

'OK, but you really do sound like one.'

'Are we going to drop the politics?'

'Yessir. Anyway: Aurelio Di Blasi, son of Giacomo and Maria Antonietta née Carlentini, born in Vigàta on April 3, 1937—'

'You get on my nerves when you talk that way. You sound like a clerk at the records office.'

'You don't like it, Chief? What do you want me to do, sing it? Recite it like poetry?'

'You know, as for being obnoxious, you're doing a pretty good job yourself this morning.'

The telephone rang.

'At this rate we'll be here till midnight.' Fazio sighed.

'H'lo, Chief? I got that Signor Càcano that called before onna line. Whaddo I do?'

'Let me talk to him.'

'Inspector Montalbano? This is Gillo Jàcono. I had the pleasure of meeting you at Mrs Vasile Cozzo's house once. I'm a former student of hers.'

Over the receiver, in the background, Montalbano heard a female voice announcing the last call for the flight to Rome.

'I remember very well. What can I do for you?'

'Excuse me for being so brief, but I'm at the airport and have only a few seconds.'

Brevity was something the inspector was always ready to excuse, at any time and under any circumstance.

'I'm calling about the woman who was murdered.'

'Did you know her?'

'No, but on Wednesday evening, about midnight, I was on my way from Montelusa to Vigàta in my car when the motor started acting up, and so I began driving very slowly. When I was in the Tre Fontane district, a dark Twingo passed me and then stopped in front of a house a short distance ahead. A man and a woman got out and walked up the drive. I didn't see anything else, but I'm sure about what I saw.'

'When will you be back in Vigàta?'

'Next Thursday.'

'Come in and see me. Thanks.'

Montalbano drifted off. That is, his body remained seated, but his mind was elsewhere.

'What should I do, come back in a little bit?' Fazio asked in resignation.

'No, no. Go ahead and talk.'

'Where was I? Ah, yes. Construction engineer, but not a builder himself. Resides in Vigàta, Via Laporta number eight, married to Teresa Dalli Cardillo, housewife, but a well-to-do housewife. Husband owns a large plot of farmland at Raffadali in Montelusa province, complete with farmhouse, which he refurbished. He's got two cars, a Mercedes and a Tempra, two children, male and female. The female's name is Manuela, thirty years old, married to a businessman and living in Holland. They've got two children, Giuliano, age three, and Domenico, age one. They live—'

'Now I'm going to break your head,' said Montalbano.

'Why? What did I do?' Fazio asked disingenuously. 'I thought you said you wanted to know everything about everything!'

The phone rang. Fazio could only groan and look up at the ceiling.

'Inspector. This is Emanuele Licalzi. I'm calling from Rome. My flight was two hours late leaving Bologna and so I missed the connection to Palermo. I'll be there at about three this afternoon.'

'No problem, I'll be expecting you.'

He looked at Fazio and Fazio looked at him.

'How much more of this bullshit have you got?'

'I'm almost done. The son's name is Maurizio.'

Montalbano sat up in his chair and pricked up his ears.

'He's thirty-one years old and a university student.'

'At thirty-one?'

'At thirty-one. Seems he's a little slow in the head. He lives with his parents. End of story.'

'No, I'm sure that is not the end of the story. Go on.'

'Well, they're only rumours . . .'

'Doesn't matter.'

Fazio was obviously having a great time playing this game with his boss, since he held all the cards.

'Well, Engineer Di Blasi is the second cousin of Dr Emanuele Licalzi. Michela became like one of the Di Blasi family. And Maurizio lost his head over her. For everyone in town, it turned into a farce: whenever Mrs Licalzi went walking around Vigàta, there he was, following behind her, with his tongue hanging out.'

So it was Maurizio's name Anna didn't want to give him.

'Everyone I spoke to,' Fazio continued, 'told me he's a gentle soul, and a little dense.'

'All right, thanks.'

'There's one more thing,' said Fazio, and it was clear he was about to fire the final blast, the biggest in the fireworks display. 'Apparently the kid has been missing since Wednesday evening. Got that?'

*

'Hello, Pasquano? Montalbano here. Got any news for me?'

'A few things. I was about to call you myself.'

'Tell me everything.'

'The victim hadn't eaten dinner. Or very little, at least, maybe a sandwich. She had a gorgeous body, inside and out. In perfect health, a splendid machine. She hadn't drunk anything or taken any drugs. Death was caused by asphyxiation.'

'Is that it?'

'No. She'd clearly had sexual intercourse.'

'Was she raped?'

'I don't think so. She'd had very rough vaginal intercourse, intense, I suppose you could say. But there was no trace of seminal fluid there. Then she'd had anal intercourse, also very rough, and again no seminal fluid.'

'But how can you know she wasn't raped?'

'Quite simple. To prepare for anal penetration an emollient cream was used, probably one of those moisturizing creams women keep in the bathroom. Have you ever heard of a rapist worried about minimizing his victim's pain? No, trust me: the lady consented. And now I have to let you go. I'll give you more details as soon as possible.'

The inspector had an exceptional photographic memory. Closing his eyes, he put his head in his hands and concentrated. A moment later he could clearly see the little jar of moisturizing cream with the lid lying beside it, the last item on the right-hand side of the messy bathroom's shelf.

✻

The nameplate next to the intercom outside Via Laporta 8 said only, 'Eng. Aurelio Di Blasi'. He rang, and a woman's voice answered.

'Who is it?'

Better not put her on her guard. They were probably already on pins and needles.

'Is Engineer Di Blasi there?'

'No, but he'll be back soon. Who is this?'

'I'm a friend of Maurizio's. Could I come in?'

For a moment he felt like a piece of shit, but it was his job.

'Top floor,' said the voice.

The lift door was opened by a woman of about sixty, dishevelled and looking very upset.

'You're a friend of Maurizio's?' the woman asked anxiously.

'Sort of,' replied Montalbano, feeling the shit spill out over his collar.

'Please come in.'

She led him into a large, tastefully furnished living room, pointed him towards an armchair, while she herself sat down in a plain chair, rocking her upper body back and forth, silent and desperate. The shutters were closed, some miserly shafts of light filtering through the slats. Montalbano felt as if he were attending a wake. He even thought the deceased was there, though invisible, and that his name was Maurizio. Scattered on the coffee table were a dozen or so photos that all showed the same face, but in the shadowy room one couldn't make out the features. The inspector heaved a long sigh, the way one does before holding one's breath to go underwater, for he was about to dive into the abyss of sorrow that was the mind of Mrs Di Blasi.

'Have you heard from your son?'

It was clear as day that things were exactly as Fazio had said.

'No. Everyone's been looking for him over land and sea. My husband, his friends ... Everyone.'

She started weeping quietly, tears running down her face, falling onto her skirt.

'Did he have much money on him?'

'Half a million lire, for certain. He also had a card, how's it called? An ATM card.'

'Let me get you a glass of water,' said Montalbano, standing up.

'Please don't bother, I'll get it myself,' the woman said, standing up in turn and leaving the room. In a flash Montalbano seized one of the photos, glanced at it – a horse-faced kid with expressionless eyes – and stuck it in his jacket pocket. Apparently Mr Di Blasi had had them made to be passed around. Mrs Di Blasi returned, but instead of sitting back down, she remained standing in the arch of the doorway. She'd become suspicious.

'You're quite a bit older than my son. What did you say your name was?'

'Actually, Maurizio is friends with my younger brother, Giuseppe.'

He'd chosen one of the most common names in Sicily. But the signora's thoughts were already elsewhere. She sat down and resumed rocking back and forth.

'So you've had no news of him since Wednesday evening?'

'None whatsoever. He didn't come home that night.

He'd never done that before. He's a simple boy, good-hearted. If you tell him dogs can fly, he'll believe you. At some point that morning, my husband got worried and started making phone calls. A friend of his had seen him walking by in the direction of the Bar Italia. It was probably nine in the evening.'

'Did he have a mobile phone?'

'Yes. But who are you, anyway?'

'Well,' the inspector said. 'I think I'll go now.'

He headed quickly for the door, opened it, then turned round.

'When was the last time Michela came here?'

Mrs Di Blasi turned red in the face.

'Don't you mention that slut's name to me!'

And she slammed the door behind him.

*

The Bar Italia was practically next door to police headquarters. Everyone, Montalbano included, was family there. The owner was sitting at the cash register. He was a big man with ferocious eyes that contrasted with his innate kindheartedness. His name was Gelsomino Patti.

'What'll it be, Inspector?'

'Nothing, Gelso. I need some information. Do you know this Maurizio Di Blasi?'

'Did they find him?'

'Not yet.'

'His dad, poor guy, has come by here at least ten times to ask if there's any news. But what kind of news could there be? If he comes back, he's going to go home, he ain't going to come and sit down at the bar.'

'Listen, Pasquale Corso—'

'Inspector, the father told me the same thing, that Maurizio came here round nine that night. But the fact is, he stopped on the street, right here in front, and I seen him real good from the register. He was about to come in, and then he stopped, pulled out his mobile phone, and started talking. A little while later he was gone. On Wednesday evening, he didn't come in here, that much I know for sure. What reason would I have for sayin' something that wasn't true?'

'Thanks, Gelso. So long.'

✻

'Chief! Dr Latte called from Montelusa.'

'Lattes, Cat, with an *s* at the end.'

'Chief, one *s* more or less don' make no difference. He said as how you should call 'im 'mediately. And then Guito Sarah Valli called after 'im. Left me 'is number in Bolonia. I wrote it on this here piece a paper.'

It was time to eat, but he could squeeze in one call.

'Hello? Who's this?'

'Inspector Montalbano. I'm calling from Vigàta. Are you Mr Guido Serravalle?'

'Yes, Inspector. I've been trying to reach you all morning, because when I called the Jolly to talk to Michela I found out...'

A warm, mature voice, like a crooner's.

'Are you a relative?'

He'd always found it to be a good tactic to pretend, during an investigation, that he knew nothing about the relationships between the various persons involved.

'No. Actually, I...'

'Friend?'

'Yes, a friend.'

'How much?'

'I'm sorry, I don't understand.'

'How much of a friend?'

Guido Serravalle hesitated before answering. Montalbano came to his aid.

'An intimate friend?'

'Well, yes.'

'So, what can I do for you?'

More hesitation. Apparently the inspector's manner was throwing him off.

'Uh, I just wanted to tell you ... to make myself available. I own an antique shop in Bologna that I can close whenever I want. If you need me for anything, I'll get on a plane and come down. I wanted ... I was very close to Michela.'

'I understand. If I need you for anything, I'll have someone ring you.'

He hung up. He hated people who made useless phone calls. What could Guido Serravalle tell him that he didn't already know?

*

He headed out on foot to have lunch at the Trattoria San Calogero, where the fish was always the freshest. All of a sudden he stopped, cursing the saints. He'd forgotten that the trattoria was closed for six days for kitchen renovations. He went back, got in his car, and drove towards Marinella. Just past the bridge, he noticed the house that he now knew belonged to Anna Tropeano. The urge got the better of him and he pulled up, stopped the car and got out.

It was a two-storey house, very well maintained, with a little garden all around. He approached the gate and pressed the button on the intercom.

'Who is it?'

'Inspector Montalbano. Am I disturbing you?'

'No, please come in.'

The gate opened, and at the same time, so did the front door of the house. Anna had changed her clothes and recovered her normal skin tone.

'You know something, Inspector? I was sure I would see you again before the day was over.'

SEVEN

'Were you eating lunch?'

'No, I'm not hungry. And anyway, all alone like this ... Michela used to come and eat here almost every day. She hardly ever had lunch at the hotel.'

'May I make a suggestion?'

'Come inside, in the meantime.'

'Would you like to come to my house? It's right here, just a stone's throw away.'

'Maybe your wife doesn't like surprise visitors ...'

'I live alone.'

Anna Tropeano didn't have to think twice about it.

'I'll meet you in your car.'

They rode in silence: Montalbano still surprised at having invited her, Anna clearly amazed with herself for having accepted.

Saturday was the day Adelina, the housekeeper, customarily devoted to a fastidious clean-up of the whole house. Seeing it so spick and span, Montalbano took comfort. Once on a Saturday he'd invited a married couple over, before Adelina had been. In the end, his friend's wife, just to set the table, had to clear away the mountain of dirty socks and underwear he'd left there for the house-keeper to wash.

As if she were already long familiar with the house, Anna went directly to the veranda, sat down on the bench, and looked out at the sea a short distance away. Montalbano set a folding table and an ashtray in front of her and went into the kitchen. Adelina had left him a large serving of haddock; in the refrigerator he found a sauce of anchovies and vinegar to add to it.

He went back out on the veranda. Anna was smoking and seemed more and more relaxed with each passing minute.

'It's so beautiful here.'

'Listen, would you like a little baked haddock?'

'Inspector, please don't be offended, but my stomach's in a knot. Let's do this: while you're eating, I'll have a glass of wine.'

*

Half an hour later, the inspector had gobbled up the triple serving of haddock and Anna had knocked back two glasses of wine.

'This is really good,' said Anna, refilling her glass.

'My father makes it ... used to make it. Would you like some coffee?'

'I won't turn down a coffee.'

The inspector opened a can of Yaucono, prepared the *napoletana*, and put it on the gas burner. He returned to the veranda.

'Please take this bottle away from me or I'll drink the whole thing,' said Anna.

Montalbano complied. The coffee was ready. He served it. Anna drank, savouring it in little sips.

'This is delicious. So strong. Where do you buy it?'

'I don't. A friend sends me a tin now and then from Puerto Rico.'

Anna pushed the cup away and lit her twentieth cigarette.

'What do you have to tell me?'

'There are some new developments.'

'What?'

'Maurizio Di Blasi.'

'You see? I didn't give you his name this morning because I knew you'd find it out with ease. He was the laughing stock of the whole town.'

'Fell head over heels for her?'

'Worse. Michela had become an obsession for him. I don't know if anyone told you, but Maurizio isn't right in the head. He's on the borderline between normal and mentally unstable. You know, there were two episodes where...'

'Tell me about them.'

'Once Michela and I went out to eat at a restaurant. A

little while later Maurizio arrived. He said hi and sat down at the table next to ours. But he ate very little and just stared at Michela the whole time. Then he suddenly started drooling and I nearly threw up. He was really drooling, believe me; he had a string of saliva hanging out of the side of his mouth. We had to leave.'

'And the other episode?'

'I'd gone up to the house to give Michela a hand. At the end of the day, she went to take a shower and afterwards came downstairs into the living room naked. It was very hot. She liked to go around the house with nothing on. Then she sat down in an armchair and we started talking. At a certain point, I heard a kind of moan coming from outside. I turned around to look. There was Maurizio, his face practically pasted against the window. Before I could say a word, he took a few steps back, bending over. And that's when I realized he was masturbating.'

She paused a moment, looked at the sea, and sighed.

'Poor kid,' she said under her breath.

Montalbano, for a moment, felt moved. That astonishing, wholly feminine capacity for deep understanding, for penetrating one's feelings, for being at once mother and lover, daughter and wife. He placed his hand on top of Anna's and she did not pull it away.

'Do you know he's disappeared?'

'Yes, I know. The same night as Michela. But...'

'But?'

'Inspector, can I speak to you frankly?'

'Why, what have we been doing up to now? But do me a favour, please call me Salvo.'

'If you call me Anna.'

'OK.'

'You know, you're wrong if you think Maurizio could ever have murdered Michela.'

'Give me one good reason.'

'Reason's got nothing to do with it. You know, people don't talk very willingly to the police. But if you, Salvo, were to conduct a poll, all of Vigàta would tell you Maurizio's not a murderer.'

'Anna, there's another development I haven't mentioned.'

Anna closed her eyes. She'd intuited that what the inspector was about to tell her would be hard to say and hard to hear.

He told her, without looking her in the face, gazing out at the sea. He didn't spare her any details.

Anna listened with her face in her hands, her elbows on the folding table. When the inspector had finished, she stood up, pale as a ghost.

'I need a bathroom.'

'I'll show you where it is.'

'I can find it myself.'

A few moments later, Montalbano heard her vomiting. He glanced at his watch; he still had an hour before

Emanuele Licalzi's visit. And, anyway, Mr Orthopedist from Bologna could certainly wait.

She returned with an air of determination and sat back down beside Montalbano.

'Salvo, what does the word "consent" mean to this pathologist?'

'The same thing it means to you or me: to agree to something.'

'But in certain cases one might appear to consent to something because there's no chance of resistance.'

'I know.'

'So I ask you: couldn't the murderer have done what he did to Michela without her wanting him to?'

'But there are certain details—'

'Forget them. First of all, we don't even know whether the killer abused a living woman or a corpse. Anyway, he had all the time in the world to arrange things in such a way that the police would lose their heads over it.'

Neither of them seemed to notice how familiar they'd become with each other.

'You're thinking something but not saying it,' said Anna.

'No, I have no problem saying it,' said Montalbano. 'At the moment, everything points to Maurizio. He was last seen at nine p.m. in front of the Bar Italia. Calling someone on his mobile phone.'

'Me,' said Anna.

The inspector literally jumped up from the bench.

'What did he want?'

'He was asking about Michela. I told him we'd parted shortly after seven, and that she would be stopping at the hotel before going to dinner at the Vassallos.'

'And what did he say?'

'He hung up without even saying goodbye.'

'That could be another point against him. He must have phoned the Vassallos next. Not finding her there, he guessed where she might be and caught up with her.'

'At the house.'

'No. They didn't arrive at the house until just after midnight.'

This time it was Anna's turn to jump.

'A witness told me,' Montalbano continued.

'He recognized Maurizio?'

'It was dark. He only saw a man and a woman get out of the Twingo and walk towards the house. Once inside, Maurizio and Michela make love. At a certain point Maurizio, who you say is a bit psycho, has an attack.'

'Never in a million years would Michela—'

'How did your friend react to Maurizio's stalking?'

'It bothered her. Sometimes she felt deeply sorry for . . .'

She stopped, realizing what Montalbano meant. Suddenly her face lost its freshness, and wrinkles appeared at the corners of her mouth.

'There are, however, a few things that don't make

sense,' said Montalbano, who suffered seeing her suffer. 'For example: would Maurizio have been capable, immediately after killing her, of coolly conceiving of stealing her clothes and bag to throw the police off the scent?'

'Are you kidding?'

'The real problem isn't finding out the details of the murder, but knowing where Michela was and what she did between the moment you left her and when the witness saw her. That's almost five hours, a pretty long time. And now we have to go because Dr Emanuele Licalzi is coming.'

As they were getting in the car, Montalbano, like a squid, squirted a black cloud over the whole picture.

'I'm not so sure your public opinion poll would be so unanimous on Maurizio's innocence. One person, at least, would have serious doubts.'

'Who?'

'His father, Engineer Di Blasi. Otherwise he would have had us out searching for his son.'

'It's natural for you to follow every lead. Oh, I just remembered something. When Maurizio rang me to ask about Michela, I told him to call her directly on her mobile phone. He said he'd already tried, but her phone was turned off.'

*

In the doorway to headquarters, he practically ran into Galluzzo, who was coming out.

'Back from your heroic exploit?'

'Yessir,' Galluzzo said uneasily. Fazio must have told him about his morning outburst.

'Is Inspector Augello in his office?'

'No sir.'

Galluzzo's uneasiness visibly increased.

'And where is he? Out clubbing other strikers?'

'He's in the hospital.'

'Eh? What happened?' Montalbano asked, worried.

'Hit on the head with a stone. They gave him three stitches. But they wanted to keep him there for observation and told me to come back at eight tonight. If everything's all right, I'll drive him home.'

The inspector's string of curses was interrupted by Catarella.

'Chief, Chief! First of all, Dr Latte with an s at the end called two times. He says as how you're asposta call him poissonally back straightaway. Then there was tree other phone calls I wrote down on dis little piece a paper.'

'Wipe your arse with it.'

✳

Dr Emanuele Licalzi was a diminutive man in his sixties, with gold-rimmed glasses and dressed all in grey. He looked as if he'd just been pressed, shaved and manicured. Impeccable.

'How did you get here?'

'You mean from the airport? I rented a car and it took me almost three hours.'

'Have you already been to your hotel?'

'No. I've got my suitcase in the car. I'll go there afterwards.'

How could he be so wrinkle-free?

'Shall we go to the house? We can talk in the car, that way you'll save time.'

'As you wish, Inspector.'

They took the doctor's rented car.

'Did one of her lovers kill her?'

He didn't beat around the bush, this Emanuele Licalzi.

'We can't say yet. One thing is certain: she had repeated sexual intercourse.'

The doctor didn't flinch, but kept on driving, calm and untroubled, as if it wasn't his wife who'd just been killed.

'What makes you think she had a lover here?'

'Because she had one in Bologna.'

'Ah.'

'Yes, Michela even told me his name. Serravalle, I think. An antiquarian.'

'That's rather unusual.'

'She used to tell me everything. She really trusted me.'

'And did you also tell your wife everything?'

'Of course.'

'An exemplary marriage,' the inspector commented ironically.

Montalbano sometimes felt irretrievably left behind by the new lifestyles. He was a traditionalist. For him, an 'open relationship' meant nothing more than a husband and wife who cheated on each other and even had the gall to tell each other what they did under or on top of the covers.

'Not an exemplary marriage,' the unflappable Dr Licalzi corrected him, 'but a marriage of convenience.'

'For Michela or you?'

'For both of us.'

'Could you explain?'

'Certainly.'

He turned right.

'Where are you going?' the inspector asked. 'This road won't take you to Tre Fontane.'

'Sorry,' said the doctor, beginning a complex manoeuvre to turn the car round. 'But I haven't been down here for a year and a half, ever since I got married. Michela saw to all the construction herself; I've only seen photographs. Speaking of photographs, I packed a few of Michela in my suitcase. I thought they might be of some use to you.'

'You know what? The murder victim might not even be your wife.'

'Are you serious?'

'Yes. Nobody has officially identified the body, and none of the people who've seen it actually knew her when she was alive. When we've finished here, I'll talk to the pathologist about identifying her. How long do you plan on staying?'

'Two, three days at the most. I want to take Michela back to Bologna.'

'Doctor, I'm going to ask you a question, and I won't ask you again. Where were you Wednesday evening, and what were you doing?'

'Wednesday? I was at the hospital, operating late into the night.'

'You were telling me about your marriage.'

'Yes. Well, I met Michela three years ago. Her brother, who lives in New York now, had a rather severe compound fracture in his foot, and she brought him to the hospital. I liked her at once. She was very beautiful, but what struck me most was her character. She was always ready to see the bright side of things. She lost both her parents before the age of fifteen and was brought up by an uncle who one day saw fit to rape her. To make a long story short, she was desperate to find a place to live. For years she was the mistress of an industrialist, but he eventually disposed of her with a tidy sum of money that helped her get along for a while. Michela could have had any man she wanted, but, basically, it humiliated her to be a kept woman.'

'Did you ask Michela to become your mistress, and she refused?'

For the first time, a hint of a smile appeared on Emanuele Licalzi's impassive face.

'You're on the wrong track entirely, Inspector. Oh, by the way, Michela told me she'd bought a bottle-green Twingo to get around town. Do you know what's become of it?'

'It had an accident.'

'Michela never did know how to drive.'

'Your wife was entirely without fault in this case. The car was properly parked in front of the drive to the house and somebody ran into it.'

'And how do you know this?'

'It was us, the police, who ran into it. At the time, however, we still didn't know—'

'What an odd story.'

'I'll tell it to you sometime. Anyhow, it was the accident that led us to discover the body.'

'Do you think I could have the car back?'

'I don't see any reason why not.'

'I could resell it to somebody in Vigàta who deals in used cars, don't you think?'

Montalbano didn't answer. He didn't give a shit about what happened to the car.

'That's the house there on the right, isn't it? I think I recognize it from the photograph.'

'That's it.'

Dr Licalzi executed an elegant manoeuvre, pulled up in front of the drive, got out of the car, and stood looking at the house with the detached curiosity of a sightseer.

'Nice. What did we come here for?'

'I don't really know, truth be told,' Montalbano said grumpily. Dr Licalzi knew how to get on his nerves. He decided to shake him up a little.

'You know, some people think it was Maurizio Di Blasi, the son of your cousin the engineer, who killed your wife.'

'Really? I don't know him. When I came here two and a half years ago, he was in Palermo for his studies. I'm told the poor boy's a half-wit.'

So there.

'Shall we go inside?'

'Wait, I don't want to forget.'

He opened the boot of the car, took out the elegant suitcase that was inside, and removed a large envelope from it.

'The photos of Michela.'

Montalbano slipped it in his jacket pocket. As he was doing this, the doctor extracted a bunch of keys from his own pocket.

'Are those to the house?'

'Yes. I knew where Michela kept them at our place in Bologna. They're the extra set.'

Now I'm going to start kicking the guy, thought the inspector.

'You never finished telling me why your marriage was as convenient for you as it was for your wife.'

'Well, it was convenient for Michela because she was marrying a rich man, even if he was thirty years older, and it was convenient for me because it put to rest certain rumours that were threatening to harm me at a crucial moment of my career. People had started saying I'd become a homosexual, since nobody'd seen me socially with a woman for more than ten years.'

'And was it true you no longer frequented women?'

'Why would I, Inspector? At age fifty I became impotent. Irreversibly.'

EIGHT

'Nice,' said Dr Licalzi again after having a look around the living room.

Didn't he know how to say anything else?

'Here's the kitchen,' the inspector said, adding, 'Eat in.'

All of a sudden he felt enraged at himself. How did that 'eat in' slip out? What was it supposed to mean? He felt like an estate agent showing a house to a prospective client.

'Next to it is the bathroom. Go and have a look yourself,' he said rudely.

The doctor didn't notice, or pretended not to notice, the tone of voice. He opened the bathroom door, stuck his head in for the briefest of peeks and reclosed it.

'Nice.'

Montalbano felt his hands trembling. He distinctly saw the newspaper headline: POLICE INSPECTOR GOES SUDDENLY BERSERK, ATTACKS HUSBAND OF MURDER VICTIM.

'Upstairs there's a small guest room, a large bathroom and the main bedroom. Go up.'

The doctor obeyed. Montalbano remained downstairs in the living room, lit a cigarette, and took the envelope of photographs of Michela out of his pocket. Gorgeous. Her face, which he had only seen distorted in pain and horror, had a smiling, open expression.

Finishing his cigarette, he realized the doctor hadn't come back down.

'Dr Licalzi?'

No answer. He bounded up the stairs. The doctor was standing in a corner of the bedroom, hands covering his face, shoulders heaving as he sobbed.

The inspector was mystified. This was the last reaction he would have expected. He went up to Licalzi and put a hand on his back.

'Try to be brave.'

The doctor shrugged him off with an almost childish gesture and kept on weeping, face hidden in his hands.

'Poor Michela! Poor Michela!'

It wasn't put on. The tears, the sorrowful voice, were real.

Montalbano took him firmly by the arm.

'Let's go downstairs.'

The doctor let himself be led, moving away without looking at the bed, the shredded, bloodstained sheet. He was a physician, and he knew what Michela must have felt during her last moments alive. But if Licalzi was a physician, Montalbano was a policeman, and as soon as he saw him in tears, he knew the man would no longer be able to maintain the mask of indifference he'd put on. The armour of detachment he customarily wore, perhaps to compensate for the disgrace of impotence, had fallen apart.

'Forgive me,' said Licalzi, sitting down in an armchair. 'I didn't imagine ... It's just horrible to die like that. The killer held her face down against the mattress, didn't he?'

'Yes.'

'I was very fond of Michela, very. She had become like a daughter to me, you know.'

Tears started streaming down his face again, and he wiped them away, without much success, with a hand-kerchief.

'Why did she decide to build this house here instead of somewhere else?' the inspector asked.

'She had always mythologized Sicily, without ever knowing the place. The first time she came for a visit, she became enchanted with it. I think she wanted to create a refuge for herself here. See that little display cabinet? Those are her things in there, personal trinkets she brought down with her from Bologna. It says a lot about her intentions, don't you think?'

'Do you want to check and see if anything's missing?'

The doctor got up and went over to the display cabinet.

'May I open it?'

'Of course.'

The doctor stared at it a long time, then raised a hand and picked up the old violin case, opened it, showed the inspector the instrument that was inside, reclosed it, put it back in its place, and shut the door.

'At a glance, there doesn't seem to be anything missing.'

'Did your wife play the violin?'

'No, she didn't play the violin or any other instrument. It belonged to her maternal grandfather from Cremona, who made them. And now, Inspector, if it's all right with you, I want you to tell me everything.'

Montalbano told him everything, from the accident on Thursday morning to what Dr Pasquano had reported to him.

Emanuele Licalzi, when it was over, remained silent for a spell, then said only two words, 'Genetic finger-printing.'

'I'm not really up on scientific jargon.'

'Sorry. I was referring to the disappearance of her clothes and shoes.'

'Might be a decoy.'

'Maybe. But it might also be that the killer felt he had no choice but to get rid of them.'

'Because he'd soiled them?' asked Montalbano, thinking of Signora Clementina's thesis.

'The coroner said there was no trace of seminal fluid, right?'

'Yes.'

'That reinforces my hypothesis, that the killer didn't

want to leave the slightest biological trace that could be used in DNA testing – that's what I meant by genetic fingerprinting. Real fingerprints can be wiped away, but what can you do about semen, hair, skin? The killer tried to make a clean sweep.'

'Right,' said the inspector.

'Excuse me, but if you don't have anything else to tell me, I'd like to leave this place. I'm starting to feel tired.'

The doctor locked the front door with his key, Montalbano put the seals back in place, and they left.

'Have you got a mobile phone?'

The doctor handed him his. The inspector called Pasquano, and they decided on ten o'clock the following morning for identifying the body.

'Will you come, too?'

'I should, but I can't. I have an engagement outside of Vigàta. I'll send one of my men for you, and he can take you there.'

He had Licalzi drop him off at the first houses on the outskirts of town. He needed a little walk.

＊

'Chief! Chief! Dr Latte with an *s* at the end called tree times, more and more pissed off each time, with all due respect. You're asposta call 'im 'mediately in poisson.'

'Hello, Dr Lattes? Montalbano here.'

'Thank heavens! Come to Montelusa immediately, the commissioner wants to talk to you.'

He hung up. It must be something serious, since the Caffè-Lattes wasn't even lukewarm.

As he was turning the key in the ignition, he saw a squad car pull up with Galluzzo at the wheel.

'Any news of Inspector Augello?'

'Yeah, the hospital called to say they were discharging him. I went and picked him up and drove him home.'

To hell with the commissioner and his urgency. He stopped at Mimì's first.

'How are you feeling, you intrepid defender of capital?'

'My head feels like it could burst.'

'That'll teach you.'

Mimì Augello was sitting in an armchair, head bandaged, face pale.

'I once got clobbered on the head by some guy with a blackjack. They had to give me seven stitches, and I still wasn't in as bad a shape as you.'

'I guess you thought you took your clobbering for a worthy cause. You got to feel clobbered and gratified at the same time.'

'Mimì, when you put your mind to it, you can be a real arsehole.'

'You too, Salvo. I was going to phone you tonight to tell you I don't think I'm in any condition to drive tomorrow.'

'We'll go to your sister's another time.'

'No, you go ahead, Salvo. She was so insistent on seeing you.'

'But do you know why?'

'I haven't the slightest idea.'

'Listen, tell you what. I'll go, but I want you to go to the Hotel Jolly tomorrow morning at nine thirty to pick up Dr Licalzi, who arrived today, and take him to the mortuary. OK?'

*

'How *are* you, old friend? Eh? You look a bit down. Chin up, old boy. *Sursum corda!* That's what we used to say in the days of Azione Cattolica.'

The Caffè-Lattes had warmed up dangerously. Montalbano began to feel worried.

'I'll go and inform the commissioner at once.'

He vanished, then reappeared.

'The commissioner's momentarily unavailable. Come, let me show you into the waiting room. Would you like a coffee or something else to drink?'

'No, thank you.'

Dr Lattes, after flashing him a broad, paternal smile, disappeared. Montalbano felt certain the commissioner had condemned him to a slow and painful death. The garrotte, perhaps.

On the table in the dismal little waiting room there was a magazine, *Famiglia Cristiana*, and a newspaper,

L'Osservatore Romano, manifest signs of Dr Lattes's presence in the commissioner's office. He picked up the magazine and began reading an article on Susanna Tamaro.

'Inspector! Inspector!'

A hand was shaking his shoulder. He opened his eyes and saw a uniformed policeman.

'The commissioner is waiting for you.'

Jesus! He'd fallen into a deep sleep. Looking at his watch, he saw that it was eight o'clock. The fucker had made him wait two hours.

'Good evening, Mr Commissioner.'

The noble Luca Bonetti-Alderighi didn't answer, didn't even say 'Shoo' or 'Get out of here', but only continued staring at a computer screen. The inspector contemplated his superior's disturbing hairdo, which was very full with a great big tuft in the middle that curled back like certain turds deposited in the open country. An exact replica of the coif of that criminally insane psychiatrist who'd triggered all the butchery in Bosnia.

'What was his name?'

It was too late when he realized that, still dazed from sleep, he'd spoken aloud.

'What was whose name?' asked the commissioner, finally looking up at him.

'Never mind,' said Montalbano.

The commissioner kept looking at him with an expression that combined contempt and commiseration,

apparently discerning unmistakable signs of senile demen-
tia in the inspector.

'I'm going to speak very frankly, Montalbano. I don't
have a very high opinion of you.'

'Nor I of you,' the inspector replied bluntly.

'Good. At least things are clear between us. I called
you here to tell you that I'm taking you off the Licalzi
murder case. I've handed it over to Panzacchi, captain of
the Flying Squad, to whom the investigation should have
fallen by rights in the first place.'

Ernesto Panzacchi was a loyal follower whom Bonetti-
Alderighi had brought with him to Montelusa.

'May I ask you why, though I couldn't care less?'

'You committed a foolish act that created a serious
impediment for Dr Arquà.'

'Did he write that in his report?'

'No, he didn't write it in his report. He very generously
didn't want to damage your career. But then he repented
and told me the whole story.'

'Ah, these repenters!' commented the inspector.

'Do you have something against repenters?'

'Let's drop it.'

He left without even saying goodbye.

'I'm going to take disciplinary measures!' Bonetti-
Alderighi shouted at his back.

*

The forensics laboratory was located in the building's basement.

'Is Dr Arquà in?'

'He's in his office.'

Montalbano barged in without knocking.

'Hello, Arquà. I'm on my way to the commissioner's, he wants to see me. Thought I'd drop in and see if you have any news for me.'

Vanni Arquà was obviously embarrassed. But since Montalbano had led him to believe he hadn't yet seen the commissioner, he decided to answer as if he didn't know the inspector was no longer in charge of the investigation.

'The murderer cleaned everything very carefully. We found a lot of fingerprints, but they clearly had nothing to do with the homicide.'

'Why not?'

'Because they were all yours, Inspector. You continue to be very, very careless.'

'Oh, listen, Arquà. Did you know that it's a sin to rat on someone? Ask Dr Lattes. You'll have to repent all over again.'

*

'Hey, Chief! Mr Cacano called another time again! Said as how he 'membered somethin's might be maybe impor'ant. I wrote 'is number down on dis here piece a paper.'

Eyeing the little square of paper, Montalbano felt his body start to itch all over. Catarella had written the numbers down in such a way that a three might be a five or a nine, the two a four, the five a six, and so on.

'Hey, Cat! What kind of number is this, anyway?'

'That's the number, Chief. Cacano's number. What's written down.'

Before reaching Gillo Jàcono, he spoke to a bar, the Jacopetti family and one Dr Balzani.

By the fourth attempt, he was very discouraged.

'Hello? Who'm I speaking with? This is Inspector Montalbano.'

'Ah, Inspector, it's very good you called. I was on my way out.'

'You were looking for me?'

'A certain detail came back to me, I'm not sure if it'll be of any use to you. The man I saw getting out of the Twingo and walk towards the house with a woman had a suitcase in his hand.'

'Are you sure about that?'

'Absolutely.'

'An overnight bag?'

'No, Inspector, it was pretty big. But...'

'Yes?'

'I had the impression the man was carrying it without effort, as if there wasn't much in it.'

'Thank you, Mr Jàcono. Please call me when you get back.'

He looked up the Vassallos' number in the phone book and dialled it.

'Inspector! I came to your office as we'd agreed, but you weren't there. I waited a while, and then I had to go.'

'Please forgive me. Listen, Mr Vassallo, last Wednesday evening, when you were waiting for Mrs Licalzi to come to dinner, did anybody call you?'

'Well, a friend of mine from Venice did, and so did our daughter, who lives in Catania – I'm sure that's of no interest to you. But, in fact, what I wanted to tell you this afternoon was that Maurizio Di Blasi did call twice that evening. Just after nine o'clock, and again just after ten. He was looking for Michela.'

*

The unpleasantness of his meeting with the commissioner needed to be blotted out with a solemn feast. The Trattoria San Calogero was closed, but he remembered a friend telling him that right at the gates to Joppolo Giancaxio, a little town about twenty kilometres inland from Vigàta, there was an *osteria* that was worth the trouble. He got in his car, and found the place immediately: it was called La Cacciatora. Naturally, they had no game. The owner-cashier-waiter, who had a big handlebar moustache and vaguely resembled the Gentleman King, Victor Emmanuel II, started things off by putting a hefty serving of delicious *caponata* in front of him. 'A joyous start is the best of guides,' wrote Boiardo, and Montalbano decided to let himself be guided.

'What will you have?'

'Bring me whatever you like.'

The Gentleman King smiled, appreciating the vote of confidence.

As a first course, he served him a large dish of macaroni in a light sauce dubbed *foco vivo* or 'live fire' (olive oil, garlic, lots of hot red pepper, salt), which the inspector was forced to wash down with half a bottle of wine. For the second course, he ate a substantial portion of lamb *alla cacciatora* that had a pleasant fragrance of onion and oregano. He closed with a ricotta cheesecake and small glass of anisette as a viaticum and boost for his digestive system. He paid the bill, a pittance, and exchanged a handshake and smile with the Gentleman King.

'Excuse me, who's the cook?'

'My wife.'

'Please give her my compliments.'

'I will.'

On the drive back, instead of heading towards Montelusa, he turned onto the road for Fiacca, which brought him home to Marinella from the direction opposite the one he usually took when coming from Vigàta. It took him half an hour longer, but in compensation he avoided passing in front of Anna Tropeano's house. He was certain he would have stopped, there was no getting around it, and he would have cut a ridiculous figure in the young woman's eyes. He phoned Mimì Augello.

'How are you feeling?'

'Terrible.'

'Listen, forget what I said to you. You can stay at home tomorrow morning. Since the matter's no longer in our hands, I'll send Fazio to accompany Dr Licalzi.'

'What do you mean, it's no longer in our hands?'

'The commissioner took the case away from me. Passed it on to the captain of the Flying Squad.'

'Why did he do that?'

'Because two does not equal three. Want me to tell your sister anything?'

'Don't tell her they broke my head open, for Christ's sake, or she'll think I'm on my deathbed.'

'Take care, Mimì.'

*

'Hello, Fazio? Montalbano here.'

'What's wrong, Chief?'

He told him to pass all phone calls relating to the case on to the Montelusa Flying Squad, and he explained what he was supposed to do with Licalzi.

*

'Hello, Livia? Salvo here. How are you doing?'

'All right, I guess.'

'What's with this tone? The other night you hung up on me before I had a chance to say anything.'

'You phoned me in the middle of the night!'

'But it was the first free moment I had!'

'Poor thing! Allow me to point out that you, between

thunderstorms, shoot-outs and ambushes, have very cleverly managed to avoid answering the very specific question I asked you last Wednesday evening.'

'I wanted to tell you I'm going to see François tomorrow.'

'With Mimì?'

'No, Mimì was hit—'

'Oh my God! Is it serious?'

She and Mimì had a soft spot for each other.

'Let me finish! He was hit on the head with a stone. Chickenshit, three stitches. So I'm going to go alone. Mimì's sister wants to talk to me.'

'About François?'

'Who else?'

'Oh my God. He must be sick. I'm going to phone her right away!'

'Come on, those people go to bed at sunset! I'll phone you tomorrow evening, as soon as I get home.'

'Let me know. I mean it. I'm not going to sleep a wink tonight.'

NINE

To go from Vigàta to Calapiano, anyone with any sense, and with an even superficial knowledge of Sicilian roads, would first have taken the superhighway to Catania, exited onto the road that turns back inland towards Troìna at 1,120 metres' elevation, descended to Gagliano at 751 metres by way of a sort of mule track that received its first and last layer of tarmac fifty years ago in the early days of regional autonomy, and finally reached Calapiano via a provincial road that clearly refused to be known as such, its true aspiration being to resume the outward appearance of the earthquake-ravaged country trail it had once been. But that wasn't the end of it. The farm belonging to Mimì's sister and her husband was four kilometres outside town, and one reached it by following a winding strip of gravel on which even goats had doubts about setting a single one of their four available hooves. This was what one might call, for lack of a better term, the best route, the one Mimì Augello always took, its difficulties and discomforts not coming entirely to the fore until the final stretch.

Naturally, Montalbano did not take it. He chose instead to cut across the island, and thus found himself, from the start, travelling roads along which the few surviving peasants interrupted their labours to gaze in amazement at the car passing recklessly by. They would talk about it at home in the evening with their children, 'Know what? This mornin' a car drove by!'

This, however, was the Sicily the inspector liked best: harsh, spare in vegetation, on whose soil it seemed (and was) impossible to live, and where he could still run across, though more and more rarely, a man in gaiters and cap, rifle on shoulder, who would raise two fingers to his visor and salute him from the back of a mule.

The sky was clear and bright and openly declared its determination to remain so until evening. It was almost hot. But the open windows did not prevent the interior of the car from becoming permeated with the delightful aromas filtering out of the packages large and small literally stuffed into the backseat. Before leaving, Montalbano had stopped at the Caffè Albanese, which made the best pastries in all of Vigàta, and bought twenty cannoli, fresh out of the oven, ten kilos' worth of *tetù, taralli, viscotti regina* and Palermitan *mostaccioli* – all long-lasting cookies – as well as some marzipan fruits, and, to crown it all, a colourful *cassata* that weighed five kilos all by itself.

He arrived in the early afternoon and worked out that

the journey had taken him more than four hours. The big farmhouse looked empty to him; only the smoking chimney said there was someone at home. He tooted his horn, and a moment later Franca, Mimì's sister, appeared in the doorway. She was a blonde Sicilian over forty, a strong, tall woman. She eyed the car, which she didn't recognize, as she wiped her hands on her apron.

'It's Montalbano,' said the inspector, opening the car door and getting out.

Franca ran up to him with a big smile on her face and embraced him.

'Where's Mimì?'

'At the last minute he couldn't come. He felt really bad about it.'

Franca looked at him. Montalbano was unable to tell a lie to people he respected; he would stammer, blush and look away.

'I'm going to phone Mimì,' Franca said decisively, walking back into the house. By some miracle Montalbano managed to load himself up with all the packages, big and small, and followed her inside a few minutes later.

Franca was just hanging up.

'He's still got a headache.'

'Reassured now? Believe me, it was nothing,' said the inspector, unloading the parcels onto the table.

'And what's this?' said Franca. 'Are you trying to turn this place into a pastry shop?'

She put the sweets in the fridge.

'How are you, Salvo?'

'Fine. And how's everybody here?'

'We're all fine, thank God. And you won't believe François. He's shot right up, getting taller by the day.'

'Where are they?'

'Out and about. But when I ring the bell for lunch, they'll all come running. Are you staying the night with us? I prepared a room for you.'

'Thanks, Franca, but you know I can't. I have to leave by five at the latest. I can't be like your brother and race along these roads like a madman.'

'Go and wash, then.'

He returned fifteen minutes later, refreshed. Franca was setting the table for nine people. The inspector decided this was perhaps the right moment.

'Mimì said you wanted to talk to me.'

'Later, later,' Franca said brusquely. 'Hungry?'

'Well, yes.'

'Want a little wheat bread? I took it out of the oven less than an hour ago. Shall I prepare you some?'

Without waiting for an answer, she cut two slices from a loaf, dressed them in olive oil, salt and black pepper, adding a slice of pecorino cheese, put this all together to form a sandwich, and handed it to him.

Montalbano went outside, sat down on a bench next to the door, and, at the first bite, felt forty years younger. He was a little kid again. This was bread the way his grandmother used to make it for him.

It was meant to be eaten in the sun, while thinking of nothing, only relishing being in harmony with one's body, the earth, and the smell of the grass. A moment later he heard shouting and saw three children chasing after each other, pushing and trying to trip one another. They were Giuseppe, nine years old, his brother, Domenico, namesake of his uncle Mimì and the same age as François, and François himself.

The inspector gazed at him, wonderstruck. He'd become the tallest of the lot, the most energetic and pugnacious. How the devil had he managed to undergo such a metamorphosis in the two short months since the inspector had last seen him?

Montalbano ran over to him, arms open wide. François, recognizing him, stopped at once as his companions turned and headed towards the house. Montalbano squatted down, arms still open.

'Hi, François.'

The child broke into a sprint, swerving around him.

'Hi,' he said.

The inspector watched him disappear into the house. What was going on? Why had he read no joy in the little boy's eyes? Montalbano tried to console himself; maybe it was some kind of childish resentment; François probably felt neglected by him.

*

At the two ends of the table sat the inspector and Aldo Gagliardo, Franca's husband, a man of few words who was as hale and hearty as his name. To Montalbano's right sat Franca, followed by the three children. François was the farthest away, sitting next to Aldo. To his left were three youths around twenty years of age, Mario, Giacomo and Ernst. The first two were university students who earned their daily bread working in the fields; the third was a German passing through who told Montalbano he hoped to stay another three months. The lunch, consisting of pasta with sausage sauce and a second course of grilled sausage, went rather quickly. Aldo and his three helpers were in a hurry to get back to work. They all pounced on the sweets the inspector had brought. Then, at a nod of the head from Aldo, they got up and went out.

'Let me make you another coffee,' said Franca. Montalbano felt uneasy. He'd seen Aldo exchange a fleeting glance of understanding with his wife before leaving. Franca served the coffee and sat down in front of the inspector.

'It's a serious matter,' she began.

At that exact moment François came back in with a resolute expression on his face, hands clenched in fists at his sides. He stopped in front of Montalbano, looked him long and hard in the eye, and said in a quavering voice, 'You're not going to take me away from my brothers.'

Then he turned and ran out. It was a heavy blow. Montalbano felt his mouth go dry. He said the first thing that came into his head, and unfortunately it was something stupid.

'His Italian's become so good!'

*

'What I was going to say, well, the boy just said it,' said Franca. 'And, mind you, both Aldo and I have done nothing but talk to him about Livia and you, and how eventually he's going to live with the two of you, and how much you all love each other, and how much more you'll all love each other one day. But there was nothing doing. The idea entered his head without warning one night about a month ago. I was sleeping, and then I felt something touch my arm. It was him.

' "You feel sick?"

' "No."

' "Then what's wrong?"

' "I'm afraid."

' "Afraid of what?"

' "That Salvo's going to come and take me away."

'And every now and then, when he's playing, when he's eating, the thought will pop into his head, and he'll turn all gloomy and even start misbehaving.'

Franca kept on talking, but Montalbano was no longer listening. He was lost in a memory from the time he was the same age as François, actually one year younger. His grandmother was dying, his mother had fallen gravely ill (though he didn't realize these things until later), and his father, to take better care of them, had taken him to the house of his sister Carmela, who was married to the owner of a chaotic shop, a kind, mild man named Pippo Sciortino. They didn't have any children. Sometime later, his father came back to get him, wearing a black tie and, he remembered very clearly, a broad black band around his left arm. He refused to go.

'I'm not coming. I'm staying with Carmela and Pippo. My name is Sciortino now.'

He could still see the sorrowful look on his father's face, and the embarrassed expressions of Pippo and Carmela.

'... because children aren't just parcels that you can deposit here or there whenever you feel like it,' Franca concluded.

*

On the way home he took the easier route and was already back in Vigàta by nine o'clock. He decided to drop in on Mimì Augello.

'You look better.'

'This afternoon I managed to get some sleep. So, you couldn't pull the wool over Franca's eyes, eh? She called me all worried.'

'She's a very, very intelligent woman.'

'What did she want to talk to you about?'

'François. There's a problem.'

'The kid's grown attached to them?'

'How did you know? Did your sister tell you?'

'She hasn't said a thing about it to me. But is it so hard to figure out? I kind of imagined it would turn out this way.'

Montalbano made a dark face.

'I can understand how you might feel hurt,' said Mimì, 'but who's to say it's not actually a stroke of luck?'

'For François?'

'For François, too. But, above all, for you, Salvo. You're not cut out to be a father, not even an adoptive father.'

✳

Just past the bridge, he noticed that the lights were on in Anna's house. He pulled up and got out of the car.

'Who is it?'

'Salvo.'

Anna opened the door and showed him into the dining room. She was watching a movie, but immediately turned off the television.

'Want a little whisky?'

'Sure. Neat.'

'You down?'

'A little.'

'It's not easy to stomach.'

'No, it's not.'

He thought a moment about what Anna had just said to him: it's not easy to stomach. How on earth did she know about François?

'But, Anna, how did you find out?'

'It was on TV, on the evening report.'

What was she talking about?

'What station?'

'TeleVigàta. They said the commissioner had assigned the Licalzi murder case to the captain of the Flying Squad.'

Montalbano started laughing.

'You think I give a shit about that? I was talking about something else!'

'Then tell me why you're feeling down.'

'I'll tell you another time. I'm sorry.'

'Did you ever meet Michela's husband?'

'Yeah, yesterday afternoon.'

'Did he tell you about his unconsummated marriage?'

'You knew?'

'Yes, Michela had told me about it. She was very fond of him, you know. But in those circumstances, taking a lover wasn't really a betrayal. The doctor knew about it.'

The phone rang in another room. Anna went and answered, then returned in an agitated state.

'That was a friend. She heard that about half an hour ago, this captain of the Flying Squad went to the home of Engineer Di Blasi and brought him into Montelusa headquarters. What do they want from him?'

'Simple. They want to know where Maurizio is.'

'So they already suspect him!'

'It's the most obvious thing, Anna. And Captain Ernesto Panzacchi, chief of the Flying Squad, is an utterly obvious man. Well, thanks for the whisky. Goodnight.'

'What, you're going to leave just like that?'

'I'm sorry, I'm tired. I'll see you tomorrow.'

A dense, heavy gloom had suddenly come over him.

✻

He opened the door to his home with a kick and ran to answer the telephone.

'What the fuck, Salvo! Some friend!'

He recognized the voice of Nicolò Zito, newsman for the Free Channel, with whom he had a genuine friendship.

'Is it true you're no longer on the case? I didn't report it because I wanted to check it with you first. But if it's true, why didn't you tell me?'

'I'm sorry, Nicolò, it happened late last night, and I left the house early this morning. I went to see François.'

'Want me to do anything on television?'

'No, that's all right, thanks. Oh, but here's something you don't already know that'll make up for everything. Captain Panzacchi brought Aurelio Di Blasi, the construction engineer from Vigàta, into Montelusa headquarters for questioning.'

'Did *he* kill her?'

'No, the real suspect is his son Maurizio, who disappeared the same night that Mrs Licalzi was killed. He, the kid, was madly in love with her. Oh, and another thing. The victim's husband is in Montelusa at the moment, at the Hotel Jolly.'

'Salvo, if they kick you off the police force, I'll hire you here. Watch the midnight news. And thanks. Really.'

The gloom lifted as Montalbano set down the receiver.

That would fix Captain Ernesto Panzacchi. At midnight all his moves would enter the public domain.

*

He really didn't feel like eating. He undressed, got into the shower, and stayed there a long time. Emerging, he put on a clean pair of briefs and undershirt. Now came the hard part.

'Livia.'

'Oh, Salvo, I've been waiting so long for your call! How is François?'

'He's great. He's grown a lot.'

'Did you notice the progress he's made? Every week, when I call, his Italian gets better and better. He's become so good at making himself understood, don't you think?'

'Even too good.'

Livia paid no attention; she had another pressing question.

'What did Franca want?'

'She wanted to talk to me about François.'

'Why, is he too energetic? Disobedient?'

'Livia, that's not the problem. Maybe we made a

mistake keeping him so long with Franca and her husband. The boy has grown attached to them. He told me he doesn't want to leave them.'

'He told you himself?'

'Yes, of his own free will.'

'Of his own free will! You're such an idiot!'

'Why?'

'Because they told him to say that to you! They want to take him away from us! They need free labour for their farm, the rascals!'

'Livia, you're talking nonsense.'

'No, it's true, I tell you! They want to keep him for themselves! And you're happy to turn him over to them!'

'Livia, try to be rational.'

'Oh, I'm rational, all right, I'm very rational! And I'll show you and those two kidnappers just how rational I am!'

She hung up. Without putting on any additional clothing, the inspector went and sat out on the veranda, lit a cigarette, and finally gave free rein to his melancholy. François, by now, was a lost cause, despite the fact that Franca was leaving the decision up to Livia and him. The truth of the matter, plain and unvarnished, was what Mimì's sister had said to him: children aren't parcels that you can deposit here or there whenever you feel like it. You can't not take their feelings into account. Rapisardi, the lawyer who was following the adoption proceedings for the inspector, had told him it would take another six months at least. And that would give François all the time in the world to put down roots at the Gagliardo home. Livia was crazy if she thought Franca could ever put words in the child's mouth. He, Montalbano, had got a good look at François's expression when he ran up to embrace him. He remembered those eyes well now: there was fear in them, and childish hatred. Besides, he could understand how the kid felt. He'd already lost his mother and was afraid to lose his new family. In the end, he and Livia had spent very little time with the boy; their images hadn't taken long to fade in his mind. Montalbano felt that he would never, ever have the courage to inflict another trauma on François. He had no right. Nor did Livia. The kid was lost to them for ever. For his part, he would consent to the child's remaining with Aldo and Franca, who were happy to adopt him. But now he felt cold, so he got up and went inside.

*

'Were you sleeping, Chief? Fazio here. I wanted to inform you that we held a meeting this afternoon. And we wrote a letter of protest to the commissioner. Everybody signed it, starting with Inspector Augello. Let me read it to you: "We the undersigned, as members of Central Police Headquarters of Vigàta, deplore—"'

'Wait. Did you send it?'

'Yes, Chief.'

'What a bunch of fucking idiots! You could at least have let me know before sending it!'

'Why? Before or after, what's the difference?'

'I would have talked you out of making such a stupid move!'

He cut off the connection, enraged.

*

It took him a while to fall asleep. Then an hour later he woke up, turned on the light, and sat up in bed. Something like a flash had made him open his eyes. During his visit to the crime scene with Dr Licalzi, something — a word, a sound — had seemed, well, dissonant. What was it? He lashed out at himself. 'What the fuck do you care? The case isn't yours any more.'

He turned off the light and lay back down.

'And neither is François,' he added bitterly.

TEN

The next morning, at headquarters, the staff was almost at full strength: Augello, Fazio, Germanà, Gallo, Galluzzo, Giallombardo, Tortorella and Grasso. The only one missing was Catarella, who had a legitimate excuse for his absence, attending the first class in his computer training course. Everyone was wearing a long face fit for the Day of the Dead, avoiding Montalbano as if he were contagious, not looking him in the eye. They'd been doubly offended: first by the commissioner, who'd taken the investigation away from their chief just to spite him, and, second, by their chief himself, who had reacted meanly to their letter of protest to the commissioner. Not only had he not thanked them — what can you do, the inspector was just that way — but he had called them a bunch of fucking idiots, and Fazio had told them this.

All present, therefore, but all bored to death, because, except for the Licalzi homicide, it had been two months since anything substantial had happened. For example, the

Cuffaro and Sinagra families, two criminal gangs perpetually engaged in a turf war who were in the custom of leaving behind, with near-perfect regularity, one corpse per month (one month a Cuffaro, the next month a Sinagra), seemed to have lost their enthusiasm a while back. Such indeed had been the case ever since Giosuè Cuffaro, after being arrested and having suddenly repented of his crimes, had helped lock up Peppuccio Sinagra, who, after being arrested and having suddenly repented of his crimes, had helped put away Antonio Smecca, a cousin of the Cuffaros, who, after suddenly repenting of his crimes, had pulled the plug on Cicco Lo Càrmine, of the Sinagra gang, who . . .

The only noise to be heard in Vigàta had been made the previous month, at the San Gerlando festival, by the firework display.

'The number-one bosses are all in jail!' Commissioner Bonetti-Alderighi had triumphantly exclaimed at a jam-packed press conference.

And the five-star bosses are still in place, the inspector had thought.

That morning Grasso, who had taken Catarella's place at the switchboard, was doing crossword puzzles, Gallo and Galluzzo were testing each other's mettle at the card game of *scopa*, Giallombardo and Tortorella were engrossed in a game of draughts, and the others were either reading or contemplating the wall. The place, in short, was buzzing with activity.

On his desk Montalbano found a mountain of papers

to be signed and various other matters to be dealt with. Subtle revenge on the part of his men?

*

The bomb, unexpectedly, exploded at one, when the inspector, his right arm stiffening, was considering going out to eat.

'Chief, there's a lady, Anna Tropeano, asking for you. She seems upset,' said Grasso.

'Salvo! My God! On the TV news headlines they said Maurizio's been killed!'

As there weren't any television sets at the police station, Montalbano shot out of his office, on his way down to the Bar Italia.

Fazio intercepted him.

'Chief, what's happening?'

'They killed Maurizio Di Blasi.'

Gelsomino, the owner of the bar, along with two clients, were staring open-mouthed at the television screen, where a TeleVigàta reporter was talking about the incident.

'...and during this night-long interrogation of the engineer Aurelio Di Blasi, Ernesto Panzacchi, captain of the Flying Squad, surmised that Di Blasi's son, Maurizio, a prime suspect in the Michela Licalzi murder case, might be hiding out at a country house belonging to the Di Blasi family in the Raffadali area. The father, however, maintained that his son had not taken refuge there, since he'd gone there himself to look for him the previous day. At ten o'clock this morning, Captain Panzacchi went to Raffadali with six other police officers and began a detailed search of the house, which is rather large. Suddenly one of the policemen spotted a man running along one of the slopes of the barren hill that stands almost directly behind the house. Giving chase, Captain Panzacchi and his men found the cave into which young Di Blasi had fled. After properly positioning his men outside, Captain Panzacchi ordered the suspect to come out with his hands up. Suddenly, Di Blasi came forward shouting, "Punish me! Punish me!" and brandishing a weapon in a threatening manner. One of the police officers immediately opened fire and young Maurizio Di Blasi fell to the ground, killed by a burst of automatic-weapons fire to the chest. The young man's almost Dostoyevskian entreaty of "punish me" was tantamount to a confession. Meanwhile, Aurelio Di Blasi, the father, has been enjoined to appoint himself a defence lawyer. He is expected to be charged with complicity in his son's escape, which came to such a tragic end.'

When a photo of the poor kid's horsey face appeared on the screen, Montalbano left the bar and returned to headquarters.

'If the commissioner hadn't taken the case away from you, that poor wretch would surely still be alive!' Mimì shouted angrily.

Saying nothing, Montalbano went into his office and

closed the door. There was a contradiction, big as a house, in the newsman's account. If Maurizio Di Blasi had wanted to be punished, and if he was so eager for this punishment, why was he threatening the policemen with a weapon? An armed man aiming a pistol at the people who want to arrest him doesn't want to be punished, he's trying to avoid being arrested, to escape.

'It's Fazio. Can I come in, Chief?'

To his amazement, the inspector saw Augello, Germanà, Gallo, Galluzzo, Giallombardo, Tortorella and even Grasso, enter behind Fazio.

'Fazio just talked to a friend of his on the Montelusa Flying Squad,' said Mimì Augello. Then he gestured to Fazio to continue.

'You know what he said the weapon was the kid threatened Panzacchi and his men with?'

'No.'

'A shoe. His right shoe. Before he fell, he managed to throw it at Panzacchi.'

*

'Anna? Montalbano here.'

'It couldn't have been him, Salvo! I'm sure of it! It's all a tragic mistake! You must do something!'

'Listen, that's not why I called. Do you know Mrs Di Blasi?'

'Yes. We've spoken a few times.'

'Go and see her at once. I'm very worried. I don't want her left alone with her husband in jail and her son just killed.'

'I'll go right away.'

*

'Chief, can I tell you something? That friend of mine from the Flying Squad just called back.'

'And he told you he was only kidding about the shoe, it was all a joke.'

'Exactly. Therefore it's true.'

'Listen, I'm going home now, and I think I'll stay there for the rest of the afternoon. Give me a ring if you need me.'

'Chief, you gotta do something.'

'Get off my fucking back, all of you!'

*

After the bridge, he drove straight on. He didn't feel like hearing again, this time from Anna, that he absolutely had to take action. By what right? Here's your fearless, flawless knight in shining armour! Here's your Robin Hood, your Zorro, your Night Avenger all in one: Salvo Montalbano!

His appetite was gone now. He filled a saucer with green and black olives, cut himself a slice of bread, and, while munching on these, dialled Zito's number.

'Nicolò? Montalbano here. Do you know if the commissioner has called a press conference?'

'It's set for five o'clock this afternoon.'

'You going?'

'Naturally.'

'You have to do me a favour. Ask Panzacchi what kind of weapon Maurizio Di Blasi threatened them with. Then after he tells you, ask him if he can show it to you.'

'What's behind this?'

'I'll tell you in due time.'

'Can I tell you something, Salvo? We're all convinced here that if you'd stayed on the case, Maurizio Di Blasi would still be alive.'

So Nicolò was jumping aboard, too, behind Mimì.

'Would you go and get fucked!'

'Thanks, I could use a little, it's been a while. By the way, we'll be broadcasting the press conference live.'

*

He went and sat on the veranda with the book by Denevi in his hands, but he was unable to read it. A thought was spinning round and round in his head, the same one he'd had the night before: what strange, anomalous thing had he seen or heard during his visit to the house with the doctor?

*

The press conference began at five on the dot. Bonetti-Alderighi was a maniac for punctuality ('It's the courtesy of kings,' he used to repeat whenever he had the chance, his noble lineage having apparently gone so far to his head that he now imagined it with a crown on top).

There were three of them seated behind a small table covered with green cloth: the commissioner in the middle, flanked by Panzacchi on the right and Dr Lattes on the left. Behind them, the six policemen who had taken part in the operation. While the faces of the policemen were grave and drawn, those of the three chiefs expressed moderate contentment – only moderate because somebody had been killed.

The commissioner spoke first, limiting himself to praising Ernesto Panzacchi ('a man with a brilliant future ahead of him') and briefly taking credit for having assigned the case to the captain of the Flying Squad, who had 'managed to solve it in twenty-four hours, when others, with their antiquated methods, would have taken untold days and weeks.'

Montalbano, sitting in front of the screen, took it all in without reacting, not even mentally.

Then it was Ernesto Panzacchi's turn to speak, and he repeated exactly what the inspector had heard the Tele-Vigàta newsman say earlier. He didn't dwell on the details, however, and seemed in rather a hurry to leave.

'Does anyone have any questions?' asked Dr Lattes.

Somebody raised a hand.

'Are you sure the suspect shouted "Punish me"?'

'Absolutely certain. He said it twice. They all heard it.'

He turned to the six policemen behind him, who nodded in agreement, looking like puppets on strings.

'And in a desperate tone of voice.' Panzacchi piled it on. 'Desperate.'

'What is the father accused of?' asked a second journalist.

'Being an accessory after the fact,' said the commissioner.

'And maybe more,' added Panzacchi with an air of mystery.

'Being an accomplice to murder?' ventured a third newsman.

'I didn't say that,' Panzacchi said curtly.

Finally Nicolò Zito signalled that he wanted to speak.

'What kind of weapon did Maurizio Di Blasi threaten you with?'

Of course, the journalists, who had no idea what had actually happened, didn't notice anything, but the inspector distinctly saw the six policemen stiffen and the half-smile on Captain Panzacchi's face vanish. Only the commissioner and the head of his cabinet had no perceptible reaction.

'A hand grenade,' said Panzacchi.

'Where did he get it?' Zito pressed him.

'Well, it was war surplus, but still functioning. We have a suspicion as to where he might have found it, but we need further confirmation.'

'Could we see it?'

'The forensics lab has it.'

And so ended the press conference.

*

At six thirty Montalbano called Livia. The phone rang a long time to no avail. He started to feel worried. What if she was sick? He called Giovanna, Livia's friend at work. She said Livia'd shown up at work as usual, but she, Giovanna, had noticed she looked very pale and nervous. Livia also told her she'd unplugged the telephone because she didn't want to be disturbed.

'How are things between the two of you?' Giovanna asked him.

'Not great, I'd say,' Montalbano replied diplomatically.

*

No matter what he did – whether he read a book or stared out at the sea smoking a cigarette – the question kept coming suddenly back to him, precise and insistent: what had he seen or heard at the house that hadn't seemed right?

*

'Hello, Salvo? It's Anna. I've just come from Mrs Di Blasi's. You were right to tell me to go there. Her family and friends have made a point of not coming round – you know, keeping their distance from someone with a husband in jail and a son who's a murderer.'

'How is Mrs Di Blasi?'

'How do you expect? She's had a breakdown; I had to call a doctor. Now she's feeling a little better; her husband's lawyer phoned saying he'd be released shortly.'

'They're not charging him with complicity?'

'I really can't say. I think they're going to charge him anyway, but release him on bail. Are you coming round?'

'I don't know, I'll see.'

'Salvo, you've got to do something. Maurizio was innocent, I'm sure of it, and they murdered him.'

'Anna, don't get any wild ideas.'

*

'Hullo, Chief? Zatchoo in poisson? Catarella here. The vikkim's huzbin called sayin' as how yer sposta call 'im poissonally at the Jolly t'nite roundabout ten aclack.'

'Thanks. How'd the first day of class go?'

'Good, Chief, good. I unnastood everyting. Teacha complimented me. Said peoples like me's rilly rare.'

*

An inspiration came to him shortly before eight o'clock, and he put it into action without wasting another minute. He jumped in the car and drove off in the direction of Montelusa.

*

'Nicolò's on the air,' said a secretary at the Free Channel studios, 'but he's almost finished.'

Less than five minutes later, Zito appeared, out of breath.

'I did what you said; did you see the press conference?'

'Yes, Nicolò, and I think we hit the mark.'

'Can you tell me why that grenade is so important?'

'Do you underestimate grenades?'

'Come on, tell me what's behind this.'

'I can't, not yet. Actually, you'll probably work it out very soon, but that's your business. I haven't told you anything.'

'Come on! What do you want me to say or do on the news? That's what you came here for, isn't it? By now you've become my secret director.'

'If you do it, I'll give you a present.'

He took one of the photos of Michela that Dr Licalzi had given him out of his jacket pocket and handed it to Nicolò.

'You're the only journalist who knows what the woman looked like when she was alive. The commissioner's office in Montelusa doesn't have any photos. All her IDs, driver's licence, or passport, if she had one, were in the bag that the murderer took with him. You can show this to your viewers if you want.'

Nicolò twisted up his face.

'You must want an awfully big favour. Fire away.'

Montalbano stood up, went over, and locked the door to the newsman's office.

'No,' said Nicolò.

'No what?'

'No to whatever it is you're going to ask me. If you need to lock the door, I don't want any part of it.'

'Look, if you give me a hand, afterwards I'll give you all the facts you need to create a nationwide uproar.'

Zito said nothing. He was clearly torn.

'What do you want me to do?' he finally asked in a low voice.

'To say you received phone calls from two witnesses.'

'Do they exist?'

'One does, the other doesn't.'

'Tell me only what the one who exists said.'

'No, both. Take it or leave it.'

'But you do realize that if anybody finds out I invented a witness they're liable to strike me off the register?'

'Of course. And in that case, I give you permission to say I talked you into it. That way, they'll send me home, too, and we can go and grow broad beans together.'

'Tell you what. Tell me about the fake one first. If the thing seems feasible, you can tell me about the real one afterwards.'

'OK. This afternoon, following the press conference, somebody phoned you saying he was out hunting in the area where the police shot down Maurizio Di Blasi. He said that things did not happen the way Panzacchi said.

Then he hung up without leaving his name. He was clearly upset and afraid. You tell your viewers you're mentioning this episode only in passing and nobly declare that you don't lend it much weight, since it was, in fact, an anonymous phone call and your professional ethics do not allow you to spread anonymous rumours.'

'And in the meantime I've actually repeated it.'

'But isn't that standard procedure for you guys, if you don't mind my saying so? Throwing the stone but keeping the hand hidden?'

'I'll tell you something about that when we're through. For now, let's hear about the real witness.'

'His name is Gillo Jàcono, but you're to give only his initials, G.J., nothing more. This gentleman, shortly after midnight last Wednesday, saw the Twingo pull up by the house in Tre Fontane, and saw Michela and an unidentified man get out of the car and walk quietly towards the house. The man was carrying a suitcase. Not an overnight bag, a suitcase. Now, the question is this: why did Maurizio Di Blasi bring a suitcase when he went to rape Mrs Licalzi? Did it maybe contain clean sheets in the event they soiled the bed? Also: did the Flying Squad find this suitcase anywhere? It was certainly nowhere inside the house.'

'Is that it?'

'That's it.'

Nicolò had turned chilly. Apparently Montalbano's criticism of journalistic methods hadn't gone down well with him.

'As for my professional ethics, this afternoon, following the press conference, I received a phone call from a
hunter who told me that things had not happened the way
the police said. But since he wouldn't give me his name,
I didn't report it.'

'You're shitting me.'

'Let me call my secretary, and you can listen to the
tape recording of the call,' said the journalist, standing up.

'I'm sorry, Nicolò. There's no need.'

ELEVEN

Montalbano tossed about in bed all night, unable to fall asleep. He kept seeing the scene of Maurizio falling to the ground and managing to throw his shoe at his tormentors, the simultaneously comical and desperate gesture of a poor wretch hunted down like an animal. 'Punish me!' he had cried out, and everyone rushed to interpret that exclamation in the most obvious, reassuring manner possible. That is, punish me because I raped and killed, punish me for my sin. But what if, at that moment, he had meant something else entirely? What was going through his head? Punish me because I'm different, punish me because I loved too much, punish me for being born ... One could go on for ever, but here the inspector stopped himself, both because he didn't like to slip into cheap philosophizing, and because he had suddenly understood that the only way to exorcize that obsessive image, and that cry, lay not in generic self-questioning but in examining the facts. To do this, one path, and only one, presented itself. And at this point he managed at last to shut his eyes for a couple of hours.

*

'All of you,' he said to Mimì Augello, entering headquarters.

Five minutes later, they were all standing before him in his office.

'Make yourselves comfortable,' said Montalbano. 'This is not an official meeting, but a talk among friends.'

Mimì and two or three others sat down, while the rest remained standing. Grasso, Catarella's replacement, leaned against the door frame, listening for the phone.

'Yesterday, Inspector Augello, when he learned that Di Blasi had been killed, said something that hurt me. He said, more or less: if you'd remained on the case, today that kid would still be alive. I could have answered that it was the commissioner who'd taken the investigation away from me, and that therefore I bear no responsibility. And this, strictly speaking, is true. But Inspector Augello was right. When the commissioner summoned me and ordered me to stop investigating the Licalzi murder, pride got the better of me. I didn't protest, I didn't rebel, I basically gave him to understand that he could go and fuck himself. And in so doing, I gambled away a man's life. Because one thing's certain, none of you would ever have shot down some poor guy who wasn't right in the head.'

They'd never heard him speak this way before and everyone looked at him flabbergasted, holding their breath.

'I thought about this last night, and I made a decision. I'm going to resume the investigation.'

Who was it that applauded first? Montalbano managed to turn his emotion into sarcasm.

'I've already told you once you're a bunch of fucking idiots, don't make me say it again.' And he continued, 'The case, as of today, is closed. Therefore, if you're all in agreement, we're going to operate underwater, with only our periscope showing. But I'm warning you: if they find out about this in Montelusa, it could mean real trouble for every one of us.'

*

'Inspector Montalbano? This is Emanuele Licalzi.'

Montalbano remembered that Catarella had told him the night before that the doctor had called. He'd forgotten.

'I'm sorry, but yesterday evening I had—'

'Oh, not at all, Inspector. Especially since everything has changed since yesterday.'

'In what sense?'

'In the sense that late yesterday afternoon I'd been assured that by Wednesday morning I could leave for Bologna with my poor Michela. Then early this morning the commissioner's office phoned to tell me that they needed a postponement and the funeral would have to wait until Friday. So I've decided to leave and come back on Thursday evening.'

'Doctor, you must have heard, of course, that the investigation—'

'Yes, of course, but I wasn't referring to the investigation. Do you remember the car we mentioned briefly, the Twingo? Could I perhaps talk to someone about reselling it?'

'Tell you what, Doctor: I'll have the car brought myself to our own personal mechanic. We did the damage ourselves and it's only right we should pay for it. And if you like, I could ask the mechanic to try and find a buyer for it.'

'You're a fine man, Inspector.'

'But tell me something, sir: what will you do with the house?'

'I'm going to put that up for sale, too.'

*

'Nicolò here. QED.'

'Explain.'

'I've been summoned to appear before Judge Tommaseo at four o'clock this afternoon.'

'And what's he want from you?'

'You've got a lot of nerve! What, you get me into this mess and you can't figure it out? He's going to accuse me of having withheld valuable testimony from the police.

And if he ever finds out that I don't even know who one of the witnesses is, then the shit is really going to hit the fan. That man is liable to throw me in jail.'

'Keep me posted.'

'Right. You can come visit me once a week and bring me oranges and cigarettes.'

✶

'Listen, Galluzzo, I'm going to need your brother-in-law, the newsman for TeleVigàta.'

'I'll tell him right away, Inspector.'

Galluzzo was on his way out of the room, but curiosity got the better of him.

'Actually, if it's something I can know about too . . .'

'Gallù, not only can you know it, you've got to know it. I need your brother-in-law to collaborate with us on the Licalzi story. Since we can't work out in the open, we must take advantage of any help the private TV stations can give us. But we have to make it look like they're acting on their own. Is that clear?'

'Perfectly.'

'Think your brother-in-law'd be willing to help us?'

Gallo started laughing.

'Chief, for you, the guy would go on TV and say the moon is made out of Swiss cheese. Don't you know he's just dying of envy?'

'Who does he envy?'

'Nicolò Zito, that's who. Says you make special considerations for Zito.'

'It's true. Last night Zito did me a favour and now he's in trouble.'

'And now you want the same to happen to my brother-in-law?'

'If he's game.'

'Tell me what you want from him, it's no problem.'

'All right, you tell him what he's supposed to do. Here, take this. It's a photograph of Michela Licalzi.'

'Man, what a beauty!'

'Now, your brother-in-law must have a photo of Maurizio Di Blasi somewhere in the studio. I think I saw them broadcast one when they reported his death. I want him to show both photos, one next to the other, on the one p.m. news, and on the evening report. I want him to say that since there's a five-hour gap between when she left her friend at seven thirty on Wednesday night and when she was seen going into her house with a man shortly after midnight, your brother-in-law would like to know if anyone has any information on the movements of Michela Licalzi during that period. Better yet, if anyone saw her during that period in the company of Maurizio, and where. Is that clear?'

'Clear as day.'

'You, from this moment on, will bivouac at Tele-Vigàta.'

'What do you mean?'

'I mean you'll be there all the time, as if you were an editor. As soon as somebody comes forward with information, you show him in and talk to him. Then you report back to me.'

*

'Salvo? It's Nicolò. I'm going to have to disturb you again.'
'Any news? Did they send the carabinieri for you?'
Apparently Nicolò was in no mood for jokes.
'Can you come to the studio immediately?'

*

Montalbano was stunned to find Orazio Guttadauro, the controversial defence lawyer, legal counsel to every mafioso in the province and even outside the province, at the Free Channel studios.

'Well, if it isn't Inspector Montalbano, what a lovely sight!' said the lawyer as soon as he saw him come in. Nicolò looked a tad uncomfortable.

The inspector eyed the newsman enquiringly. Why had he summoned him there with Guttadauro? Zito responded verbally, 'Mr Guttadauro was the gentleman who phoned yesterday, the one who was hunting.'

'Ah,' said the inspector. With Guttadauro, the less one spoke, the better. He was not the kind of man one would want to break bread with.

'The words that the distinguished journalist here present,' began the lawyer in the same tone of voice he employed in court, 'used to describe me on television made me feel like a worm!'

'Good God, what did I say?' asked Nicolò, concerned.

'You used these exact words, and I quote: "unknown hunter" and "anonymous caller".'

'What's so offensive about that? There's the Unknown Soldier . . .'

'. . . and the Anonymous Venetian,' Montalbano chimed in, beginning to enjoy himself.

'What? What?' The lawyer went on as if he hadn't heard them, 'Orazio Guttadauro, implicitly accused of cowardice? I couldn't bear it, and so, here I am.'

'But why did you come to us? It was your duty to go to Captain Panzacchi in Montelusa and tell him—'

'Are we kidding ourselves, boys? Panzacchi was twenty yards away from me and told a completely different story! Given the choice between me and him, people will believe him! Do you know how many of my clients, upright citizens all, have been implicated and charged on the basis of the lying words of a policeman or carabiniere? Hundreds!'

'Excuse me, sir, but in what way is your version different from Captain Panzacchi's?' asked Zito, finally giving in to curiosity.

'In one detail, my good man.'

'Which?'

'Young Di Blasi was unarmed.'

'No, no, I don't believe it. Are you trying to tell us

that the Flying Squad shot him down in cold blood, for the sheer pleasure of killing a man?'

'I said simply that Di Blasi was unarmed. The others, however, thought he was armed, since he did have something in his hand. It was a terrible misunderstanding.'

'What did he have in his hand?' Nicolò Zito's voice had risen in pitch.

'One of his shoes, my friend.'

While the journalist was collapsing into his chair, the lawyer continued.

'I feel it is my duty to make this fact known to the public. I believe that my solemn civic duty requires ...'

Montalbano began to understand Guttadauro's game. Since it wasn't a Mafia killing, and he wouldn't, by testifying, be harming any of his clients, he had a perfect opportunity to publicize himself as a model citizen and at the same time stick it to the police.

'I'd also seen him the previous day,' the lawyer said.

'Who?' Zito and Montalbano asked together, both lost in thought until that moment.

'The Di Blasi kid, who else? The hunting's good in that area. I saw him from a distance, I didn't have binoculars. He was limping. Then he went inside the mouth of the cave, sat down in the sun, and began eating.'

'Wait a minute,' said Zito. 'Are you saying the man was hiding there and not at his own house, which was a stone's throw away?'

'What do you want me to say, my dear Zito? The day

before that, when passing in front of the Di Blasi house, I saw that the front door was bolted with a padlock the size of a trunk. I am positive that at no point did he hide out at his house. Maybe he didn't want to compromise his family.'

Montalbano was convinced of two things: the lawyer was prepared to belie the assertions of the Flying Squad captain even as concerned the young man's hideout, which meant that the charge against the father would have to be dropped, with grave prejudice to Panzacchi. As for the second thing, he needed confirmation.

'Would you tell me something, sir?'

'At your orders, Inspector.'

'Are you always out hunting? Aren't you ever in court?'

Guttadauro smiled at him. Montalbano smiled back. They had understood each other. In all likelihood, the lawyer had never gone hunting in his life. Those who'd seen the incident and sent him on this mission must have been friends of the people Guttadauro called his clients. And the objective was to create a scandal for the Montelusa police department. The inspector had to play shrewdly; he didn't like having these people as allies.

'Was it Mr Guttadauro who told you to call me?' the inspector asked Nicolò.

'Yes.'

Therefore *they* knew everything. They were aware he'd been wronged, they imagined he was determined to avenge himself, and they were ready to use him.

'You, sir, must certainly have heard that I am no longer in charge of the case, which in any event should be considered closed.'

'Yes, but—'

'There are no buts, sir. If you really want to do your duty as a citizen, go to Judge Tommaseo and tell him your version of the events. Good day.'

He turned around and walked out. Nicolò came running after him and grabbed him by the arm.

'You knew! You knew about the shoe! That's why you told me to ask Panzacchi what the weapon was!'

'Yeah, Nicolò, I knew. But I advise you not to mention it on your news programme. There's no proof that things went the way Guttadauro says, even though it's probably the truth. Be very careful.'

'But you yourself are telling me it's the truth!'

'Try to understand, Nicolò. I'd be willing to bet that our good lawyer doesn't even know where the fuck the cave that Maurizio hid in is located. He's a puppet, and his strings are pulled by the Mafia. His friends found something out and decided they could take advantage of it. They cast a net into the sea and they're hoping to catch Panzacchi, the commissioner and Judge Tommaseo in it. That would make some pretty big waves. However, to haul the net back into the boat, they need somebody strong, that is, me, who they think is blinded by the desire for revenge. Now do you get the picture?'

'Yes. What line should I take with the lawyer?'

'Repeat the same things I said. Let him go and tell it to the judge. He'll refuse, you'll see. But it's you who will repeat to Tommaseo, word for word, what Guttadauro said. If he's not a fool, and he's not, he'll realize that he, too, is in danger.'

'But he had nothing to do with the killing of Di Blasi.'

'But he signed the indictment against his father. And those guys are prepared to testify that Maurizio never hid in his father's house at Raffadali. Tommaseo, if he wants to save his arse, has to disarm Guttadauro and his friends.'

'How?'

'How should I know?'

*

Since he was in Montelusa anyway, the inspector decided to go to Montelusa Central Police Station, hoping not to run into Panzacchi. Once there, he headed immediately to the basement, where forensics was located. He walked straight into the office of the chief.

'Hello, Arquà.'

'Hello,' the other said, iceberg-cold. 'What can I do for you?'

'I was just passing by, and I became curious about something.'

'I'm very busy.'

'Of course you are, but I'll only steal a minute of your time. I want some information about the grenade Di Blasi tried to throw at those police officers.'

Arquà didn't move a muscle.

'I'm not required to tell you anything.'

How could he be so self-controlled?

'Come on, colleague, be a sport. I need only three things: colour, size and make.'

Arquà looked sincerely baffled. His eyes were clearly asking whether Montalbano hadn't gone completely mad.

'What the hell are you saying?'

'Let me help you. Black? Brown? Forty-three? Forty-four? Moccasin? Superga? Varese?'

'Calm down,' said Arquà, though there was no need. He was sticking to the rule that one should try to humour madmen. 'Come with me.'

Montalbano followed behind him. They entered a room with a big, white half-moon table around which stood three busy men in white smocks.

'Caruana,' Arquà said to one of the three men, 'show our colleague Montalbano the grenade.'

As this man was opening a metal cabinet, Arquà continued talking.

'It's dismantled now, but when they brought it here it was live and dangerous.'

He took the plastic bag that Caruana held out to him, and showed it to the inspector.

'An old OTO, issued to our army in 1940.'

Montalbano was unable to speak. He studied the pieces of the grenade as if looking at the fragments of a Ming vase that had just fallen to the floor.

'Did you take fingerprints?'

'They were very blurry for the most part, but two of Maurizio Di Blasi's came out very clearly, the thumb and index finger of the right hand.'

Arquà set the bag on the table, put his hand on Montalbano's shoulder, and pushed him out into the corridor.

'I'm sorry, it's all my fault. I had no idea the commissioner would take you off the case.'

He was attributing what he thought was a momentary lapse of Montalbano's mental abilities to the shock of his removal. A good kid, deep down, Dr Arquà.

*

The chief of the crime lab had undoubtedly been sincere, Montalbano thought as he drove down to Vigàta. He couldn't possibly be that brilliant an actor. But how can one throw a hand grenade gripping it only with the thumb and index finger? The best thing that might happen if you threw it that way is that you'd blow your balls to bits. Arquà should have been able to get a print of much of the right palm as well. Given all this, where had the Flying Squad performed the feat of taking two of the already dead Maurizio's fingers and pressing them by force against the grenade? No sooner had he posed the question, than he turned around and headed back to Montelusa.

TWELVE

'What do you want?' asked Pasquano as soon as he saw him enter his office.

'I need to appeal to our friendship,' Montalbano began.

'Friendship? You and I are friends? Do we ever dine together? Do we confide in each other?'

Dr Pasquano was like that, and the inspector didn't feel the least bit upset by his words. It was merely a matter of finding the right formula.

'Well, if not friendship, then mutual esteem.'

'That, yes.'

He'd guessed right. It would be smooth sailing from here.

'Doctor, what other tests do you have to run on Michela Licalzi? Are there any new developments?'

'New developments? I told the judge and the commissioner long ago that as far as I was concerned, we could turn the body over to the husband.'

'Oh, really? Because, see, the husband himself told me he got a call from the commissioner's office saying that the funeral couldn't be held until Friday morning.'

'That's their goddamn business.'

'Excuse me, Doctor, for taking advantage of your patience. Was everything normal with the body of Maurizio Di Blasi?'

'What do you mean?'

'Well, how did he die?'

'What a stupid question. A burst of machine-gun fire. They practically cut him in two. They could've made a bust of him and put it on a column.'

'And the right foot?'

Dr Pasquano narrowed his beady eyes.

'Why are you asking me about the right foot?'

'Because I don't find the left one very interesting.'

'Right. He hurt himself, a sprain or something, couldn't get his shoe back on. But he'd hurt himself a few days before he was killed. His face was all swollen from some kind of blow.'

Montalbano gave a start.

'Had he been beaten?'

'I don't know. He was either hit hard in the face with a stick or club or ran into something. But it wasn't the policemen. The contusion dated from some time before that.'

'From when he hurt his foot?'

'More or less, I suppose.'

Montalbano stood up and held out his hand to the doctor.

'Thank you. I'll be on my way. One last thing. Did they inform you immediately?'

'Inform me of what?'

'Of the fact they'd shot Di Blasi.'

Dr Pasquano squinted his eyes so far that he looked as if he'd suddenly fallen asleep. He didn't answer immediately.

'Do you dream these things up at night? Do the crows whisper them in your ear? Do you talk to ghosts? No, they shot the kid at six in the morning. They didn't inform me until around ten. Said they wanted to finish searching the house first.'

'One final question.'

'With all your final questions, you're going to keep me here till nightfall.'

'After they turned Di Blasi's body over to you, did anyone from the Flying Squad ask for your permission to examine it alone?'

Dr Pasquano looked surprised.

'No. Why would they do that?'

*

Montalbano returned to the Free Channel. He had to bring Nicolò Zito up to date on the latest developments. He was sure Guttadauro the lawyer would be gone by now.

'Why'd you come back?'

'Tell you in a second, Nicolò. How'd it go with the lawyer?'

'I did what you told me to do. I suggested he go and talk to the judge. He said he'd think about it. Then he added something curious, that had nothing to do with anything. Or so it seemed. You never know with these people. He said, "Lucky you, who live among images! Nowadays only images matter, not words." That's what he said. What's it mean?'

'I don't know. You know, Nicolò, they've got the grenade.'

'God! So what Guttadauro told us is untrue!'

'No, it's true. Panzacchi's a shrewd one, he's covered himself very cleverly. The crime lab's examining a grenade that Panzacchi gave them, and it's got Di Blasi's finger-prints on it.'

'Jesus, what a mess! Panzacchi's covered himself from every angle! What am I going to tell Tommaseo?'

'Exactly what we agreed on. Except you shouldn't appear too sceptical about the existence of the grenade. Understood?'

*

To get to Vigàta from Montelusa there was, aside from the usual route, a little abandoned road the inspector was very fond of. He turned onto it, and when he'd reached a small bridge spanning a torrent that had ceased being a torrent centuries ago and was now merely a depression of stones and pebbles, he stopped the car, got out, and wended his way into a thicket at the centre of which stood a gigantic Saracen olive tree, one of those twisted, gnarled ones that creep along the ground like snakes before ascending to the sky. He sat down on a branch, lit a cigarette, and started meditating on the events of the morning.

✦

'Mimì, come in, close the door, and have a seat. I need some information from you.'

'Ready.'

'If I seize a weapon from someone, say, a revolver or a submachine gun, what do I do with it?'

'Usually, you give it to whoever's standing closest to you.'

'Did we wake up this morning with a sense of humour?'

'You want to know the regulations on the subject? Weapons seized must be turned immediately over to the appointed office at Montelusa Central Police Station, where they are registered and then put away under lock and key in a small depository at the opposite end of the building from the forensics lab of, in this case, Montelusa. Good enough?'

'Yes. Now, Mimì, I'm going to venture a reconstruction. If I say anything stupid, interrupt me. Here goes:

Panzacchi and his men search Engineer Di Blasi's country house. The front door, mind you, is bolted with an enormous padlock.'

'How do you know that?'

'Mimì, don't take advantage of the permission I just gave you. A padlock is not something stupid. I know it was there, period. They, however, think it might be a ruse – that is, they think Di Blasi senior, after supplying his son with provisions, locked him up inside so the house would appear uninhabited. He would go and free him after things cooled down a little. Suddenly, one of the men spots Maurizio on a nearby hillside going into the cave. They go and surround the entrance, Maurizio comes out holding something in his hand, and one of the more nervous policemen shoots and kills him. When they realize the poor bastard was holding his right shoe in his hand because he could no longer fit it on his injured foot—'

'How do you know this?'

'Mimì, if you don't knock it off, I'm going to stop telling you the story. When they see it's only a shoe, they realize they're in shit up to their necks. The brilliant operation of Ernesto Panzacchi and his dirty half dozen is in danger of creating a terrible stink. After thinking long and hard, they realize the only way out is to claim that Maurizio actually *was* armed. OK, but with what? And that's where our Flying Squad captain has a brainstorm: a hand grenade.'

'Why not a gun, which is more likely?'

'Face it, Mimì, you're just not on Panzacchi's level. The captain of the Flying Squad knows that Engineer Di Blasi doesn't have a licence to carry a gun, nor has he ever reported owning any weapons. But a war memento, which you've got before your eyes each day, is no longer considered a weapon. Or else it's packed away in an attic and forgotten.'

'May I say something? In 1940 Engineer Di Blasi was about five years old, and if he was doing any fighting, it was with a popgun.'

'What about his father, Mimì? An uncle, perhaps? A cousin? His grandfather? His great-grandfather? His—'

'OK, OK.'

'The problem is, where does one find a war-surplus hand grenade?'

'In the Montelusa police depository,' Mimì Augello said calmly.

'Right you are. And the timing fits, because they didn't notify Dr Pasquano until four hours after Maurizio's death.'

'How do you know that? OK, sorry.'

'Do you know who's in charge of the depository?'

'Yes, and you know him, too: Nenè Lofàro. He worked here with us for a while.'

'Lofàro? If I remember him correctly, he's not the kind of person to whom you can say, "Give me the key, I need a hand grenade."'

'We'll have to look into how it was done.'

'You go to Montelusa, Mimì. I can't, since I'm under fire.'

'All right. Oh, Salvo, could I have the day off tomorrow?'

'You got some whore on your hands?'

'Not a whore, a lady friend.'

'But can't you spend the evening with her, after you've finished here?'

'She said she's leaving tomorrow afternoon.'

'A foreigner, eh? All right, good luck. But first you have to unravel this story of the hand grenade.'

'Not to worry. I'll go to Montelusa today, after I eat.'

*

He felt like spending a little time with Anna, but once over the bridge, he shot past and went straight home.

In his letter box he found a large brown envelope that the postman had folded in two to make it fit. There was no return address. Feeling hungry, Montalbano opened the fridge: baby octopus *alla luciana* and a very simple fresh tomato sauce. Apparently Adelina hadn't had the time or the desire to make more. While waiting for the spaghetti water to boil, he opened the envelope. Inside was a colour catalogue for 'Eroservice', featuring pornographic videos for every single, or singular, taste. He tore it in half and tossed it into the rubbish bin. He ate and went into the bathroom, then came racing out, trousers unzipped, like a character in a silent film. How had he not thought of it sooner? Had it taken the porno catalogue? He looked up a number in the Montelusa phone book.

'Hello, Mr Guttadauro? Inspector Montalbano here. Were you eating? Yes? I'm so sorry.'

'What can I do for you, Inspector?'

'A friend of mine, talking of this and that – you know how these things happen – mentioned to me that you have an excellent collection of videos of yourself hunting.'

A very long pause. Apparently the lawyer's brain was in high gear.

'Yes, it's true.'

'Would you be willing to show me a few?'

'I'm very particular, you know, about my possessions. But we could make an arrangement.'

'That's what I was hoping you'd say.'

They said goodbye as if they were the greatest of friends. It was clear what had taken place. Guttadauro's friends – there had to be more than one – happen to witness the killing of Maurizio. When they see a policeman racing away in a squad car, they realize Panzacchi has hatched a plan for saving his face and career. One of the friends then runs and equips himself with a video camera. And he returns in time to tape the scene of the policemen pressing the dead man's fingerprints onto the hand grenade. Guttadauro's friends now have a grenade of their own, though different in nature, and they have sent the lawyer into the field. A nasty, dangerous situation, which Montalbano absolutely had to find a way out of.

*

'Mr Di Blasi? Inspector Montalbano here. I need to speak to you immediately.'

'Why?'

'Because I have serious doubts about your son's guilt.'

'He's already gone.'

'Yes, of course, sir. But his memory.'

'Do what you want.'

Utter resignation. A breathing, talking corpse.

'I'll be at your place in half an hour at the latest.'

*

He was astonished to see Anna open the door for him.

'Talk in a low voice. The signora is finally resting.'

'What are you doing here?'

'It was you who got me involved. I haven't had the heart to leave her alone since.'

'What do you mean, alone? Hasn't anyone called for a nurse?'

'Of course. But she wants me. Now come inside.'

The living room was even darker than the time the inspector was shown in by Mrs Di Blasi. He felt his heart sink when he saw Aurelio Di Blasi lying crosswise on the armchair. The man's eyes were closed, but he'd sensed the inspector's presence, and he spoke out.

'What do you want?' he asked with that terrible, dead voice.

Montalbano explained what he wanted. He spoke for half an hour straight and little by little saw the engineer sit up, prick up his ears, look at him and listen with interest. He realized he was winning him over.

'Does the Flying Squad have the keys to your villa?'

'Yes,' Mr Di Blasi said in a different, stronger voice. 'But I had a third pair made some time ago. Maurizio kept them in his bedside table. I'll go and fetch them.'

He was unable to get up from the armchair. Montalbano had to help him.

*

He blew into headquarters like a gunshot.

'Fazio, Gallo and Giallombardo, come with me.'

'Are we taking the squad car?'

'No, we'll go in mine. Is Mimì back?'

He wasn't back. They left in a hurry. Fazio had never seen him drive so fast. He got worried, not having a lot of faith in Montalbano's driving abilities.

'Want me to drive?' asked Gallo, who was apparently harbouring the same concerns as Fazio.

'Don't bust my balls. We have very little time.'

It took him about twenty minutes to drive from Vigàta

to Raffadali. Once outside the town, he turned onto a country road. Mr Di Blasi had carefully explained to him how to get to the house. They all recognized it easily, having seen it repeatedly on television.

'Now, I've got the keys,' said Montalbano. 'We're going to go inside and do a thorough search. We've still got a few hours of daylight left, and we must take advantage of it. We have to find what we're looking for before it gets dark, because we can't turn on any lights. We don't want anyone seeing the lights on from outside. Is that clear?'

'Perfectly clear,' said Fazio. 'But what are we looking for?'

The inspector told them, then added, 'I hope I'm wrong, I really do.'

'But we'll leave fingerprints,' said Giallombardo, worried. 'We didn't bring gloves.'

'We don't give a fuck.'

*

Unfortunately, the inspector hadn't been wrong. After they'd been searching for an hour, he heard Gallo call him triumphantly from the kitchen. They all came running. Gallo was stepping down from a chair, a leather ammunition box in his hand.

'It was on top of this cupboard.'

The inspector opened it: inside was a hand grenade

exactly like the one he'd seen in the crime lab, and a pistol that looked like the kind once issued to German officers.

*

'Where were you guys? What's in that case?' asked Mimì, curious as a cat.

'And what have you got to tell me?'

'Lofàro's on sick leave for a month. He was replaced fifteen days ago by somebody named Culicchia.'

'I know him well,' said Giallombardo.

'What's he like?'

'He's not the type who likes to sit behind a desk keeping records. He'd sell his soul to go back in the field. He wants to make a career of it.'

'He's already sold his soul,' said Montalbano.

'So, what's in there?' Mimì asked, increasingly curious.

'Chocolate, Mimì. Now listen, all of you. When does Culicchia go off duty? Eight o'clock, right?'

'That's right,' Fazio confirmed.

'When Culicchia leaves Montelusa Central, I want you, Fazio, and you, Giallombardo, to persuade him to get into my car. Don't explain anything to him. Keep him guessing. As soon as he's sitting down between you two, show him the ammunition box. Of course, he's never seen it before, so he's going to ask you what this whole charade is about.'

'Come on, can't somebody tell me what's in there?' Mimì asked again, but nobody answered.

'How come he won't recognize it?'

The question came from Gallo. The inspector gave him a dirty look.

'Haven't you guys got any brains in your head? Maurizio Di Blasi was retarded, but he was a decent person, and he certainly didn't have any friends who could provide him with weapons at the drop of a hat. The only place he could have found the grenade was at his country house. But they need proof that he took it from there. So Panzacchi, who's a slyboots, orders one of his men to go to Montelusa to get two grenades and one wartime pistol. One of these he'll claim was in Maurizio's hand, the other he hangs on to, together with the pistol, until he can come up with an ammo box. Then he sneaks back into the Raffadali house and hides the whole kit and caboodle in the first place where somebody would look for it.'

'So that's what's in the box!' exclaimed Mimì, slapping his forehead.

'In short, that motherfucking Panzacchi has created a perfectly plausible scenario. And if someone should ask him why the other weapons weren't found during the first search, he can claim they were interrupted when they spotted Maurizio going into the cave.'

'What a son of a bitch!' said Fazio indignantly. 'First he kills an innocent kid — because as captain he's responsible even though he didn't fire the shots himself — and now he wants to screw a poor old man just to save his own skin!'

'Let's get back to what you have to do. Let this

Culicchia simmer a little. Tell him the ammo box was found at the house in Raffadali. Then show him the grenade and the gun. Then ask him – as if out of curiosity – if all seized weapons are registered. And, finally, make him get out of the car together with you, carrying the weapons and ammo box.'

'Is that everything?'

'That's everything, Fazio. The next move is his.'

THIRTEEN

'Chief? Galluzzo's onna phone. He wants to talk to you in person. Whaddo I do, Chief? Put 'im through?'

It was clearly Catarella on the afternoon shift. But why did he say 'in person' and not 'in poisson'?

'All right, put him through. What is it, Galluzzo?'

'Inspector, some guy phoned TeleVigàta after they broadcast the photos of Mrs Licalzi and Maurizio Di Blasi together like you asked. He says he's positive he saw the lady with a man around eleven thirty that evening, but the man was not Maurizio Di Blasi. He says they stopped at his bar, right outside Montelusa.'

'Is he sure it was Wednesday night?'

'Positive. He explained that he didn't go to the bar on Monday and Tuesday because he was out of town, and Thursday it's closed. He left his name and address. What should I do, come back to the station?'

'No, stay there until after the eight o'clock news. Somebody else might come forward.'

The door flew open, slammed against the wall, and the inspector started.

'C'n I come in?' asked Catarella, smiling.

Without a doubt, Catarella had a problem with doors. Montalbano, confronted with that innocent face, suppressed the attack of nerves that had come over him.

'Yes. What is it?'

'This package jes now came f'you, and this personally 'dressed letter.'

'How's your course in pewters going?'

'Fine, Chief. But they're called computers, Chief.'

Montalbano looked at him in amazement as he left the room. They were corrupting Catarella.

Inside the envelope he found a few typewritten lines without a signature:

> *This is only the last part. Hope it's to your liking. If you want to see the whole video, call me whenever you like.*

Montalbano felt the package. A videotape.

✻

As Fazio and Giallombardo had his car, he summoned Gallo to drive him in the squad car.

'Where are we going?'

'To Montelusa, to the Free Channel studios. And don't speed, I mean it. I don't want a rerun of last Thursday.'

Gallo's face darkened.

'Aw, it happens to me once and you start bellyaching the minute you get in the car!'

They drove there in silence.

'Should I wait for you?' Gallo asked when they got there.

'Yes. This won't take very long.'

Nicolò Zito showed him into his office. He was nervous.

'How'd it go with Tommaseo?'

'How do you expect? He gave me a royal tongue-lashing, flayed me alive. He wanted the witnesses' names.'

'And what did you do?'

'I pleaded the Fifth Amendment.'

'C'mon, there's no such thing in Italy.'

'Fortunately! Since anyone who pleads the Fifth in America still gets screwed anyway.'

'How did he react when he heard Guttadauro's name? That must have had a certain effect.'

'He got all flummoxed. Looked worried to me. At any rate, he gave me an official warning. Next time he's going to throw me in jail with no questions asked.'

'That's what I wanted.'

'For me to get thrown in jail with no questions asked?'

'No, arsehole, for him to know that Guttadauro and the people he represents are mixed up in this.'

'What's Tommaseo going to do, in your opinion?'

'He'll talk to the commissioner about it. I'm sure he realizes he's caught in the net, too, and he's going to try to wiggle out of it. Listen, Nicolò, I need to watch this video.'

He handed it to him. Nicolò took it and inserted it in his VCR. It opened with a long shot showing a handful of men in the country, but their faces were unreadable. Two people in white smocks were loading a body onto a stretcher. Superimposed across the bottom of the image were the unmistakable words: 'Monday 14.4.97.' Whoever was shooting the scene then zoomed in, and now one could see Panzacchi and Dr Pasquano talking. There was no sound. The two men shook hands and the doctor walked out of the field of vision. The image then panned out to capture the six officers of the Flying Squad standing around their captain. Panzacchi said a few words to them, and they all walked off camera. End of show.

'Holy shit!' Zito said under his breath.

'Make me a copy.'

'I can't do it here, I have to go into the production studio.'

'All right, but be careful: don't let anyone see it.'

> I've viewed the sample. It's of no interest. Do whatever you like with it. But I advise you to destroy it or use it in strictest privacy.

Montalbano didn't sign the note or write down the address, which he knew from the phone directory.

Zito returned and handed him two tapes.

'This is the original and this is the copy. It came out only so-so. You know how it is, making a copy of a copy...'

'I'm not competing for an Oscar. Give me a big brown envelope.'

He slipped the copy in his jacket pocket and put the note and original in the envelope. He didn't write any address on this, either.

Gallo was in the car, reading the *Gazzetta dello Sport*.

'Do you know where Via Xerri is? At number eighteen you'll find the law offices of Orazio Guttadauro. I want you to drop off this envelope, then come back and get me.'

*

When Fazio and Giallombardo straggled back into headquarters, it was past nine.

'Oh, Inspector, what a farce, and a tragedy, too!' said Fazio.

'What did he say?'

'First he talked, and then he didn't,' said Giallombardo.

'When we showed him the ammo box, he didn't understand. He said, "What's this? Some kind of joke, eh? Is this a joke?" As soon as Giallombardo told him the box had been found at Raffadali, his face changed and started to turn pale.'

'Then, when he saw the weapons inside,' interjected

Giallombardo, who wanted to put in his two cents, 'he had a fit, and we were scared he was going to have a stroke right there in the car.'

'He was shaking all over, like he had malaria. Then he got up, climbed over me and ran away in a hurry,' said Fazio.

'He was running like an injured hare, stepping this way and that,' concluded Giallombardo.

'What now?' asked Fazio.

'We've made our noise. Now we wait for the echo. Thanks for everything.'

'Duty,' Fazio said dryly. And he added, 'Where should I put the ammo box? In the safe?'

'Yes,' said Montalbano.

Fazio had a rather large safe in his room. It wasn't used for documents, but for holding seized drugs or weapons before turning them over to Montelusa.

*

Fatigue sneaked up on him; his forty-sixth was just around the corner. He informed Catarella he was going home, but told him to forward any phone calls to him. Past the bridge he stopped the car, got out, and walked up to Anna's house. And what if she was with someone? He tried anyway.

Anna greeted him.

'Come on in.'

'Anybody there?'

'Nobody.'

She sat him down on the sofa in front of the television, turned down the volume, left the room, and returned with two glasses, one with whisky for the inspector, another with white wine for herself.

'Have you eaten?'

'No,' said Anna.

'Don't you ever eat?'

'I ate at midday.'

Anna sat down beside him.

'Don't get too close; I can tell I smell,' said Montalbano.

'Did you have a rough afternoon?'

'Rather.'

Anna extended her arm across the back of the sofa; Montalbano leaned his head back, resting the nape of his neck against her skin. He closed his eyes. Luckily he had put the glass down on the coffee table, because he fell at once into a deep sleep, as though the whisky had been drugged. He woke up with a start half an hour later, looked all around himself in confusion, realized what had happened, and felt embarrassed.

'Forgive me.'

'Good thing you woke up. My arm is full of pins and needles.'

The inspector stood up.

'I have to go.'

'I'll see you out.'

At the door, very naturally, Anna placed her lips lightly on Montalbano's.

'Have a good sleep, Salvo.'

*

He took a very long shower, changed his underwear and clothes, and phoned Livia. The phone rang for a long time, then the connection was suddenly cut off. What was that blessed woman doing? Was she wallowing in her sorrow over François? It was too late to ring her friend and get an up-date. He went and sat down on the veranda, and after a short while he decided that if he couldn't get in touch with Livia within the next forty-eight hours, he would drop everything and everyone, grab a flight to Genoa, and spend at least one day with her.

*

The ringing of the telephone had him running in from the veranda. He was sure it was Livia calling him, finally.

'Hello? Am I speaking to Inspector Montalbano?'

He'd heard that voice before, but couldn't remember who it belonged to.

'Yes. Who's this?'

'This is Ernesto Panzacchi.'

The echo had arrived.

'What is it?'

Were they on familiar terms or not? At this point it didn't matter.

'I want to talk to you. In person. Should I come to your place?'

He had no desire to see Panzacchi in his house.

'I'll come to you. Where do you live?'

'At the Hotel Pirandello.'

'I'm on my way.'

*

Panzacchi's room at the hotel was as big as a ballroom. Aside from a king-size bed and an armoire, it had two armchairs, a large table with television and VCR on top, and a minibar.

'There hasn't been time yet for my family to move down here.'

At least they'll be spared the trouble of moving twice, the inspector thought.

'Excuse me, I have to take a piss.'

'Look, there's nobody in the bathroom.'

'I really do need to piss.'

There was no trusting a snake like Panzacchi. When Montalbano returned from the bathroom, Panzacchi invited him to sit down in one of the armchairs. The captain of the Flying Squad was a stocky but elegant man with very pale blue eyes and a Tatar-style moustache.

'Can I get you something?'

'Nothing.'

'Should we get right to the point?' Panzacchi asked.

'As you like.'

'Well, a patrolman came to see me this evening, a certain Culicchia, I don't know if you know him.'

'Personally, no, by name, yes.'

'He was literally terrified. Apparently two men from your station threatened him.'

'Is that what he said?'

'That's what I believe I understood.'

'You understood wrong.'

'Then you tell me.'

'Listen, it's late and I'm tired. I went into the Di Blasis' house in Raffadali, looked around a little, and with very little effort found an ammunition box with a hand grenade and a pistol inside. I've got them in my safe now.'

'Jesus Christ! You've got no authorization!' said Panzacchi, standing up.

'You're going down the wrong road,' Montalbano said calmly.

'You're concealing evidence!'

'I said you're on the wrong road. If we keep talking about authorization and going by the book, I'm going to get up, walk out of that door and leave you behind in the shit. Because that's where you are, deep in shit.'

Panzacchi hesitated a moment, weighed the pros and cons, and sat back down. He'd given it a shot, and the first round had gone badly for him.

'You should even thank me,' the inspector went on.

'For what?'

'For having taken the ammunition box out of the

house. It was supposed to prove where Maurizio Di Blasi found his hand grenade, right? Except that forensics wouldn't have found Di Blasi's fingerprints in there even if their lives depended on it. And how would you have explained that? By saying Maurizio had worn gloves? Can you imagine the laughter!'

Panzacchi said nothing, his pale eyes looking straight into the inspector's.

'Shall I go on? Your first sin ... actually, no, I don't give a fuck about your sins, the first mistake you made was to hunt down Maurizio before being absolutely certain of his guilt. But you wanted to carry out a "brilliant" operation at all costs. Then what happened happened, and you breathed a real sigh of relief. Pretending you were saving one of your men who mistook a shoe for a weapon, you concocted the story of the hand grenade, and to make it more credible, you went and planted the ammo box in the Di Blasi house.'

'That's all talk. If you go and say those things to the commissioner, rest assured he won't believe a word of it. You're spreading these rumours just to tarnish my reputation, to avenge yourself for the fact that the investigation was taken away from you and turned over to me.'

'And what are you going to do about Culicchia?'

'He's coming with me to the Flying Squad offices tomorrow morning. I'll pay the price he's asking.'

'And what if I take the weapons to Judge Tommaseo?'

'Culicchia'll say it was you who asked him for the key

to the depository the other day. He's ready to swear by it. Try to understand: he has to defend himself, and I suggested to him how to do this.'

'So I've lost?'

'It looks that way.'

'Does that VCR work?'

'Yes.'

'Could you play this tape?'

Montalbano took it out of his pocket and handed it to Panzacchi who didn't ask any questions, but simply inserted the cassette. The images appeared, the captain of the Flying Squad watched them all the way through, then rewound the tape, extracted the cassette, and handed it to Montalbano. He sat down and lit a half-consumed Tuscan cigar.

'That's just the last part. I've got the whole tape in the same safe as the weapons,' Montalbano lied.

'How did you do it?'

'I didn't make the tape myself. There were two men in the area who saw what was going on and filmed it. Friends of Guttadauro, the lawyer, whom you know well.'

'This is a nasty development, totally unexpected.'

'It's a lot nastier than you can possibly imagine. It so happens you're being squeezed between me and them.'

'Allow me to say that their reasons I can understand perfectly well; it's yours that don't seem so clear to me, unless you're motivated by feelings of revenge.'

'Now you try to understand *my* position. I cannot,

under any circumstances, allow the captain of the Montelusa Flying Squad to become a hostage of the Mafia. I
can't let you be subject to blackmail.'

'Look, Montalbano, all I wanted to do was protect the
good name of my men. Can you imagine what would have
happened if the press had discovered we killed a man who
was defending himself with a shoe?'

'Is that why you implicated Maurizio's father, who had
nothing to do with the case?'

'With the case, no, but with my plan, yes. As for
possible attempts at blackmail, I know how to defend
myself.'

'I'm sure you do. You can hold out, which isn't a very
nice way to live, but what about Culicchia and the other
six who'll be put under pressure every single day? How
long will they hold out? All you need is for one to crack,
and the whole story comes out. I'll give you a very likely
scenario: As soon as they get sick of your refusals, the
mob is liable to give a public viewing of their tape or
send it to a private TV station that'll jump at the scoop
even if it means risking prison. And if that happens, the
commissioner gets fried too.'

'What should I do?'

Montalbano looked at him in admiration for a
moment. Panzacchi was a ruthless, unscrupulous player,
but he knew how to lose.

'You should disarm them, neutralize the weapon
they've got in their hands.' He couldn't resist adding a

malicious comment he immediately regretted. 'This is not a shoe,' he said. 'Talk about it, tonight, with the commissioner. Find a solution together. But I warn you: if you haven't made a move by twelve tomorrow, I'll make my own move, in my own way.'

He got up, opened the door, and went out.

*

'I'll make my own move, in my own way.' It had a nice ring to it. Just threatening enough. But what did it really mean? If, say, the captain of the Flying Squad were to get the commissioner on his side, and the latter in turn got Judge Tommaseo to join them, he, Montalbano, was as good as fucked. But was it possible that everyone in Montelusa had suddenly become dishonest? The antipathy a particular person might arouse is one thing; his character and integrity were another matter.

He returned to Marinella full of doubts and questions. Had he been right to talk that way to Panzacchi? Would the commissioner accept that he wasn't motivated by a desire for revenge? He dialled Livia's number. As usual, no answer. He went to bed, but it took him two hours to fall asleep.

FOURTEEN

When he walked into the office, his nerves were so obviously frayed that his men judged it best to give him a wide berth. *Of all things the bed is the best. / If you can't sleep you still can rest.* So went the proverb, but it was wrong, for not only had the inspector slept only fitfully in his bed, he had also woken up feeling like he'd run a marathon.

Only Fazio, who was closest to him, ventured to ask a question, 'Any news?'

'I'll be able to tell you after twelve.'

Galluzzo came in.

'Inspector, yesterday evening I looked for you over land and sea.'

'Did you try the sky?'

Galluzzo realized this was no time for preambles.

'Inspector, after the eight o'clock news report, somebody phoned. He said that on Wednesday evening, around eight, eight fifteen at the latest, Mrs Licalzi stopped at his petrol station and filled up her tank. He left his name and address.'

'OK. We'll drive over there later.'

He was tense, unable to set his eyes on a sheet of paper, and he kept looking at his watch. What if by twelve nobody had called from Montelusa?

At eleven thirty the telephone rang.

*

'Chief,' said Grasso, 'it's Zito the newsman.'

'Let me talk to him.'

At first he didn't know what was happening.

'Bat-ta-tum, bat-ta-tum, bat-ta-tum, tum-tùm-tumtùm,' said Zito.

'Nicolò?'

'"Fratelli d'Italia, l'Italia s'è desta—"'

Zito had started singing the Italian national anthem in a booming voice.

'Come on, Nicolò, I'm not in the mood for jokes.'

'Who's joking? I'm about to read you a press release that was sent to me just a few minutes ago. Plant your arse firmly in your chair. For your information, this was sent to us, to TeleVigàta, and to five different newspaper correspondents. I quote:

Montelusa Police Commissioner's Office.

For strictly personal reasons, Ernesto Panzacchi has asked to be relieved of his responsibilities as captain of the Flying Squad and to be placed on reserve. His request has been granted. Mr Anselmo Irrera will temporarily assume the position vacated by Captain Panzacchi. As some new and unexpected developments have emerged in the Licalzi murder case, Inspector Salvo Montalbano of Vigàta police will assume charge of the investigation for its duration.

Signed: Bonetti-Alderighi,
Montelusa Police Commissioner.

'We won, Salvo!'

Montalbano thanked his friend and hung up. He did not feel happy. The tension had dissipated, of course; he'd got the answer he wanted. Still, he felt a kind of malaise, a profound uneasiness. He cursed Panzacchi sincerely, not for what he'd done, but for having forced him to act in a way that now troubled him.

The door flew open, the whole staff rushed in. 'Inspector!' said Galluzzo. 'My brother-in-law phoned just now from TeleVigàta, they just got a press release—'

'I know, I've already been told.'

'We're going to go out and buy a bottle of spumante and . . .'

Giallombardo, withering under Montalbano's gaze, didn't finish the sentence. They all filed out slowly, muttering under their breath. He had one foul disposition, that inspector . . .

*

Judge Tommaseo didn't have the courage to show his face to Montalbano and pretended to be going over some important papers, bent over his desk. The inspector imagined that at that moment the judge wished he looked like the Abominable Snowman, with a beard covering his entire face, though Tommaseo's bulk fell short of the yeti's.

'You must understand, Inspector. As far as withdrawing the weapons possession charge, there's no problem, I've already called Mr Di Blasi's lawyer. But it's not quite so easy for me to lift the complicity charges. Until proved to the contrary, Maurizio Di Blasi is self-convicted of the murder of Michela Licalzi. My prerogatives in no way permit me to—'

'Good day,' said Montalbano, getting up and walking out.

Judge Tommaseo came running after him along the corridor.

'Inspector, wait! I want to clarify—'

'There is nothing at all to clarify, Your Honour. Have you spoken with the commissioner?'

'Yes, at great length. We met at eight o'clock this morning.'

'Then you must surely be aware of certain details of no importance to you. Such as the fact that the investigation of the Licalzi murder was conducted like a toilet-cleaning operation, that young Di Blasi was ninety-nine per cent innocent, that he was slaughtered like a pig by mistake, and that Panzacchi covered it all up. You can't dismiss the weapons charges against the engineer and at the same time not start proceedings against Panzacchi, who actually planted the weapons in his house.'

'I'm still examining Captain Panzacchi's situation.'

'Good. Examine it well. But choose the right scales, among the many you keep in your office.'

Tommaseo was about to react, but reconsidered and said nothing.

'Tell me something, for the sake of curiosity,' said Montalbano. 'Why hasn't Mrs Licalzi's body been turned over to her husband yet?'

The judge's embarrassment became more pronounced. He clenched his right hand in a fist and stuck his right index finger in it.

'Uh, that was ... yes, that was Captain Panzacchi's idea. He pointed out to me that public opinion ... In short, first the body was found, then Di Blasi died, then the funeral of Mrs Licalzi, then young Maurizio's funeral ... Don't you see?'

'No.'

'It was better to spread them out, over time ... To relieve some of the pressure on people, all the crowding...'

He was still talking, but the inspector was already at the end of the corridor.

✳

When he came out of the court building it was already two o'clock. But instead of returning to Vigàta, he took the Enna–Palermo road. Galluzzo had carefully explained to him how to find the petrol station and bar-restaurant where Michela Licalzi had been seen. The station, located just three kilometres outside Montelusa, was closed. The inspector cursed the saints, drove another two kilometres, then saw, on his left, a sign that said: TRUCKERS' BAR-TRATTORIA. As oncoming traffic was heavy, the inspector waited patiently for someone to decide to let him turn, but, seeing there was no hope in heaven, he cut right in front of everyone, amidst a pandemonium of screeching tyres, horn blasts, curses and insults, and pulled into the bar's parking lot.

It was very crowded inside. He walked up to the cashier.

'I'd like to speak with a Mr Gerlando Agrò.'

'That's me. And who are you?'

'Inspector Salvo Montalbano. You phoned TeleVigàta to say—'

'Well, goddamn it all! Did you have to come right now? Can't you see how busy I am?'

Montalbano got an idea that struck him as brilliant.

'How's the food here?'

'See those people sittin' down? They's all truckers. Ever seen a trucker go wrong?'

At the end of the meal (the idea hadn't been brilliant, but only good, the food remaining within ironclad limits of normality, with no flights of fancy), after the coffee and anisette, the cashier, who'd got a boy to take his place, approached Montalbano's table.

'Now we can talk,' he said. 'OK if I sit down?'

'Of course.'

Gerlando Agrò immediately had second thoughts.

'Maybe it's better if you come with me.'

They went out of the building.

'OK. Wednesday, around eleven thirty at night, I was here outside, smoking a cigarette, and I saw this Twingo pull in off the Enna–Palermo road.'

'Are you sure?'

'I'd bet my life on it. The car stopped right in front of me, and a lady, who was driving, got out.'

'Would also bet your life it was the same woman you saw on TV?'

'Inspector, with a woman like that, poor thing, it's hard to make a mistake.'

'Go on.'

'The man, on the other hand, stayed in the car.'

'How did you know it was a man?'

'See, there was a truck with its headlights on. I was surprised, because usually it's the man that gets out and the woman who stays in the car. Anyway, the lady ordered two salami sandwiches and bought a bottle of mineral water. My son Tanino was at the cash register, the same kid who's there now. The lady paid and went down these three steps here. But on the last step, she tripped and fell, and the sandwiches flew out of her hands. I went down the steps to help her up and I found myself face-to-face with the man, who'd got out of the car. "It's all right, it's all right," the lady said. The guy got back in the car, she ordered two more sandwiches, paid, and they drove off in the direction of Montelusa.'

'You've been very helpful, Mr Agrò. And I assume you can also say that the man you saw on television was not the same man who was in the car with the lady.'

'Definitely not. Two totally different people.'

'Where did the lady keep her money? In a large bag?'

'No sir, Inspector. She didn't have any bag. She had a little purse in her hand.'

✻

After the tension of the morning and the hearty meal he'd just eaten, fatigue came over him. He decided to go home to Marinella and sleep for an hour. Just past the bridge, however, he couldn't resist. He stopped, got out, and rang the intercom. Nobody answered. Anna had probably gone out to see Mrs Di Blasi. Perhaps it was just as well.

At home, he phoned headquarters.

'I want Galluzzo here at five with the squad car,' he said.

He dialled Livia's number, and it rang and rang to no avail. He dialled the number of her friend in Genoa.

'Montalbano here. Listen, I'm starting to get seriously worried. It's been days since—'

'Don't worry. Livia just phoned me a little while ago to let me know she was OK.'

'Where on earth is she?'

'I don't know. All I know is she called personnel and asked for another day off.'

He hung up and the phone rang.

'Inspector Montalbano?'

'Yes, who's this?'

'Guttadauro. My compliments, Inspector.'

Montalbano hung up, undressed, got into the shower, then came out and threw himself down, still naked, on the bed. He fell asleep immediately.

*

'*Riiing, riiing*,' a faraway sound chimed in his head. He realized it was the doorbell. He got up with effort, and went and opened the door. Seeing him naked, Galluzzo leaped backwards.

'What's the matter, Gallù? Think I'm going to drag you inside and make you do lewd things?'

'I've been ringing for the last half hour, Inspector. I was about to break down the door.'

'Do that and you'll have to pay for a new one. I'll be back in a second.'

*

The petrol-station attendant was a young man of about thirty with tight curls, dark, sparkling eyes and a solid, slender body. Though he was wearing overalls, the inspector could easily imagine him as a lifeguard on the beach at Rimini, playing havoc with the German girls.

'You say the lady was on her way from Montelusa, and it was eight o'clock.'

'Sure as death. I was closing up at the end of my shift. She rolled down her window and asked me if I could fill it up for her. "For you, I'll stay open all night if you want," I said. She got out of the car. Jesus, was she ever a beauty.'

'Do you remember how she was dressed?'

'All in denim.'

'Did she have any luggage?'

'She had a kind of large handbag on the back seat of the car.'

'Go on.'

'I finished filling up her tank, I told her how much she owed me, and she paid me with a one-hundred-thousand-lire bill, which she took from her purse. As I was giving her change – I like to kid around with the ladies, you see – I asked her, "Anything special I can do for you?" I sort of expected her to answer with an insult, but she just smiled and said, "For the special things I've already got someone." And she continued on her way.'

'She didn't turn back towards Montelusa? Are you sure of that?'

'Absolutely certain. The poor thing, when I think of how she ended up!'

'OK. Thanks.'

'Oh, one more thing, Inspector. She was in a hurry. After I filled up her tank, she drove off really fast. See down there? It's all straight. I watched her car till she rounded the bend. She was really speeding.'

*

'I'd planned to come home tomorrow,' said Gillo Jàcono, 'but as I got back today, I thought I'd check in with you right away.'

A distinguished man in his thirties, with a pleasant face.

'Thanks for coming.'

'I wanted to tell you that with something like this, you think about it again and again.'

'Do you want to change the statement you made over the phone?'

'Absolutely not. Although, after playing the thing over and over in my head, I would like to add one detail. But just to be safe, you probably ought to preface what I'm about to say with a very big "maybe".'

'Go ahead and talk.'

'Well, the man was carrying his suitcase without effort, in his left hand, and that's why I had the impression it wasn't very full. Whereas with his right arm he was supporting the woman.'

'Did he have his arm around her?'

'Not exactly. She was resting her hand on his arm. It

seemed to me – seemed, I repeat – as if she was limping slightly.'

*

'Dr Pasquano? Montalbano here. Am I disturbing you?'

'I was making a Y-shaped incision in a corpse. I don't think he'll mind if I stop for a few minutes.'

'Did you notice any signs on Mrs Licalzi's body that might indicate that she fell sometime before her death?'

'I don't remember. Let me take a look at the report.'

He returned before the inspector could light his cigarette.

'Yes. She'd fallen on one knee. But she was clothed at the time. In the abrasion on her left knee we found microscopic fibres from the jeans she was wearing.'

*

There was no need for further confirmation. At 8 p.m., Michela Licalzi fills her tank and heads inland. Three and a half hours later she's on her way back with a man. Sometime after midnight she's seen with a man again, certainly the same man, walking towards her house outside Vigàta.

'Hi, Anna. Salvo here. I dropped by your place early this afternoon, but you weren't there.'

'Mr Di Blasi called and said his wife was unwell.'

'I hope soon to have good news for them.'

Anna said nothing, and Montalbano realized he'd said

something stupid. The only news the Di Blasis might consider good was the resurrection of Maurizio.

'Anna, I wanted to tell you something I discovered about Michela.'

'Why don't you come over?'

No, he shouldn't. He realized that if Anna brought her lips to his another time, no good would come of it.

'I can't, Anna. I have an engagement.'

Good thing he was on the phone, because if he'd been right in front of her, she would have immediately realized he was lying.

'What did you want to tell me?'

'I have worked out, with a convincing degree of certainty, that at eight o'clock on Wednesday evening, Michela took the Enna–Palermo road. She may have been going to a town in the Montelusa province. Now, think hard before answering: as far as you know, did she have any other acquaintances in the area, aside from the people she knew in Montelusa and Vigàta?'

The answer didn't come immediately. Anna was thinking about it, as the inspector had asked.

'Look – friends, I doubt it. She'd have told me. Acquaintances, on the other hand, yes, a few.'

'Where?'

'For example, in Aragona and Comitini, which are both along that road.'

'What kind of acquaintances?'

'She bought her floor tiles in Aragona. And she got

some other supplies that I can't remember now in Comitini.'

'Therefore only business dealings.'

'I'd say so. But, you see, Salvo, you can go just about anywhere from that road. There's a turn that goes to Raffadali, for one; the captain of the Flying Squad could have spun something out of that, too.'

'Another thing: sometime after midnight, she was seen in her drive, after getting out of her car. She was leaning on a man.'

'Are you sure?'

'I'm sure.'

The pause this time was very long. So long that the inspector thought they'd been cut off.

'Are you still there, Anna?'

'Yes. Salvo, I want to repeat, clearly, once and for all, what I said before. Michela was not the kind of woman who went in for fly-by-night affairs. She confided to me that she was physically incapable of it. Will you understand that? She loved her husband. And she was very, very attached to Serravalle. She could not have consented, I don't care what the coroner thinks. She was horribly raped.'

'How do you explain that she didn't phone to let the Vassallos know she wouldn't be coming to dinner at their house? She had a mobile phone, didn't she?'

'I don't understand what you're getting at.'

'I'll explain. When Michela left you at seven thirty,

saying she was going back to the hotel, she was telling you the absolute truth at that moment. But then something happened that made her change her mind. And it can only have been a call to her mobile, since when she was travelling up the Enna–Palermo road, she was still alone.'

'You think she was on her way to an appointment?'

'There's no other explanation. It was unexpected, but she didn't want to miss that appointment. That's why she didn't call the Vassallos. She had no plausible excuse that might justify her not coming, and so the best thing was to give them the slip. Let's set aside, if you want, the possibility of an amorous rendezvous; maybe it was a work-related appointment that somehow turned tragic. I'll grant you that for the moment. But in that case I ask you: what could have been of such importance as to make her behave so rudely towards the Vassallos?'

'I don't know,' Anna said dejectedly.

FIFTEEN

What could have been so important? the inspector asked himself again after saying goodbye to his friend. If not love or sex, which in Anna's opinion were out of the question, that left only money. During the construction of the house, Michela must have handled some money, and a fair amount at that. Might the key lie hidden there? The conjecture, however, immediately seemed to him without substance, a thread in a spider's web. But he was duty-bound to investigate all the same.

'Anna? Salvo again.'

'Did your engagement fall through? Can you come over?'

There was such happiness and eagerness in the girl's voice, the inspector didn't want a note of disappointment to spoil it.

'Well, I won't say I can't make it at all.'

'Come whenever you like.'

'OK, but there's something I wanted to ask you.

Do you know if Michela opened a bank account in Vigàta?'

'Yes, it was more convenient for paying bills. It was with the Banca Popolare. But I don't know how much she had in it.'

It was too late to dash over to the bank. He opened a drawer in which he'd put all the papers he'd taken from the hotel room, and selected the dozens of bills and the little notebook of expenses. The diary and the rest of the papers he put back in the drawer. It was going to be a long, boring task, and 90 per cent certain to prove utterly useless. Besides, he was no good at numbers.

He carefully examined all the invoices. As far as he could tell at a glance, they did not appear inflated; the prices seemed to correspond to the market rates and were even occasionally a little lower. Apparently Michela knew how to bargain and save. No dice, therefore. A useless task, as he had expected. Then, by chance, he noticed a discrepancy between the amount on one bill and the round figure recorded in the notebook; the cost had been increased by five million lire. Could Michela, normally so well organized and precise, have possibly made so obvious a mistake? He started over from the top, with the patience of a saint. The end result he arrived at was that the difference between the amounts registered in the notebook and the money actually spent was one hundred and fifteen million lire.

A mistake was therefore out of the question. But if

there hadn't been a mistake, it made no sense, because it meant that Michela was taking a cut of her own money. Unless . . .

'Hello, Dr Licalzi? Inspector Montalbano here. Excuse me for calling you at home after work.'

'Yes, it's been a bad day, in fact.'

'I'd like to know something about your . . . Let me put it another way: did you and your wife have a joint bank account?'

'Inspector, weren't you—'

'Taken off the case? Yes, I was, but now everything is back to how it was before.'

'No, we didn't have a joint account. Michela had hers and I had mine.'

'Your wife had no income of her own, did she?'

'No, she didn't. We had an arrangement where every six months I would transfer a certain sum from my account into hers. If her expenses exceeded that amount, she would tell me and I'd take care of it.'

'I see. Did she ever show you the invoices concerning the house?'

'No, and I wasn't interested, really. At any rate, she recorded her expenditures one by one in a notebook. Every now and then I'd give it a look.'

'Doctor, thank you and—'

'Did you take care of it?'

What was he supposed to have taken care of? He didn't know how to answer.

'The Twingo,' the doctor helped him.

'Oh, yes, it's already been done.'

It certainly was easy to lie on the phone. They said goodbye and made an appointment to see each other on Friday morning, the day of the funeral.

Now it all made more sense. The wife was taking a cut of the money she was getting from her husband to build the house. Once the invoices were destroyed (which Michela certainly would have done had she remained alive), only the figures logged into her notebook would have remained. Just like that, one hundred and fifteen million lire had slipped into the shadows, and she had used them however she wished.

But what did she need that money for? Was somebody blackmailing her? And if so, what did Michela Licalzi have to hide?

*

The following morning, as he was about to get in his car and drive to work, the telephone rang. For a moment he was tempted not to answer. A phone call to his home at that hour could only have been an annoying, pain-in-the-arse call from headquarters.

Then the unquestionable power that the telephone has over man won out.

'Salvo?'

He immediately recognized Livia's voice and felt his legs turn to jelly.

'Livia! Finally! Where are you?'

'In Montelusa.'

What was she doing in Montelusa? When did she get there?

'I'll come and get you. Are you at the station?'

'No. If you wait for me, I'll be at your place in half an hour at the most.'

'I'll wait for you.'

What was going on? What the hell was going on? He called headquarters.

'Don't pass any calls on to me at home.'

In half an hour he downed four cups of coffee. He put the *napoletana* back on the burner. Then he heard a car pull up and stop. It must be Livia's taxi. He opened the door. It wasn't a taxi, it was Mimì Augello's car. Livia got out, the car turned around and left.

Montalbano began to understand.

She looked slovenly and dishevelled, with dark circles round her eyes, which were swollen from crying. But most of all, how had she become so tiny and fragile? A plucked sparrow. Montalbano felt overcome with tenderness and emotion.

'Come,' he said, taking her hand, leading her into the house, and sitting her down in the dining room. He saw her shudder.

'Are you cold?'

'Yes.'

He went into the bedroom, got a jacket and put it over her shoulders.

'Want some coffee?'

'All right.'

It had just boiled, and he served it piping hot. Livia drank it down as if it was cold.

*

They were sitting on the bench on the veranda. Livia had wanted to go outside. The day was so serene it looked fake. No wind, only a few light waves. Livia gazed long at the sea in silence, then rested her head on Salvo's shoulder and started crying, without sobbing. The tears streamed down her face and wet the little table. Montalbano took one of her hands; she surrendered it lifelessly to him. The inspector needed desperately to light a cigarette, but didn't.

'I went to see François,' Livia said suddenly.

'I guessed.'

'I decided not to tell Franca I was coming. I got on a plane, grabbed a taxi, and descended on them out of the blue. As soon as he saw me, François ran into my arms. He was truly happy to see me. And I was so happy to hold him and furious at Franca and her husband, and especially at you. I was convinced that everything was as I'd suspected: that you and they had been conspiring to take him away from me. And, well, I started railing against them and insulting them. All of a sudden, as I was trying to calm down, I realized that François was no longer beside me. I began to suspect they'd hidden him from me, locked him in a room somewhere, and I started to scream. I screamed so loudly that they all came running, Franca's children, Aldo, the three labourers. And they all started asking each other where François was, but nobody'd seen him. Now worried, they all went outside, calling his name. I remained alone inside, crying. Suddenly I heard a voice. "Livia, I'm here." It was him. He'd hidden somewhere inside the house, and they were all looking for him outside. See how clever and intelligent he is?'

She broke out in tears again, having held them too long inside.

'Just relax. Lie down a bit. You can tell me the rest later,' said Montalbano, who couldn't bear Livia's torment. With some effort he refrained from embracing her, sensing that this would have been the wrong move.

'But I'm leaving,' said Livia. 'My flight leaves Palermo at two this afternoon.'

'I'll drive you there.'

'No, I've already arranged it all with Mimì. He's coming by in an hour to pick me up.'

The moment Mimì walks into the office, the inspector thought, *I'm going to bust his arse so badly he won't be able to walk.*

'It was he who persuaded me to come and see you; I wanted to go home yesterday.'

Oh, so now he was supposed to thank Mimì into the bargain?

'You didn't want to see me?'

'Try to understand, Salvo. I need to be alone, to collect my thoughts, to draw some conclusions. This has all been overwhelming for me.'

The inspector felt curious to know the rest.

'Well, tell me what happened next.'

'As soon as I saw François there in the room, I instinctively drew near to him, but he moved away.'

Montalbano remembered the scene he'd endured a few days earlier.

'He looked me straight in the eye and said, "I love you, Livia, but I won't leave this house and my brothers." I sat there immobile, frozen. And he went on, "If you take me away with you, I'll run away for good and you'll never see me again." Then he ran out shouting, "I'm here, I'm here!" I started to feel dizzy, and the next thing I knew I was lying in a bed, with Franca beside me. My God, how cruel children can be sometimes!'

And wasn't what we wanted to do to him cruel? Montalbano thought.

'I felt very weak. When I tried to get up, I fainted again. Franca didn't want me to leave. She called a doctor and never left my side. I slept there. Actually slept! I spent the whole night sitting in a chair by the window. The next morning Mimì came. Her sister had phoned him. Mimì has been like a brother to me, more than a brother. He made sure I didn't run into François again. He took me out, showed me half Sicily, and he talked me into coming here, even if only for an hour. "The two of you need to talk, to explain yourselves," he said. We got to Montelusa last night, and he accompanied me to the Hotel Della Valle. This morning he came round and brought me here. My suitcase is in his car.'

'I don't think there's much to explain,' said Montalbano.

An explanation would have been possible only if Livia, realizing she'd been wrong, had expressed a word of understanding, just one, regarding his feelings. Or did she think that he, Salvo, had felt nothing when he realized they'd lost François for ever? Livia wasn't allowing for any openings, she was shut up inside her own grief and could see nothing but her own selfish despair. And what about him? Weren't they, until proven otherwise, a couple whose bond was built on love, yes, and on sex, too, but above all on a relationship of mutual understanding that bordered at times on complicity? One word too many, at that moment, might trigger an irreparable rupture. Montalbano swallowed his resentment.

'What do you intend to do?' he asked.

'About ... the boy?' She couldn't bring herself to pronounce François's name.

'Yes.'

'I won't stand in his way.'

She got up abruptly and ran towards the sea, moaning in a low voice like a mortally wounded animal. Then, unable to stand it any longer, she threw herself face down on the sand. Montalbano picked her up in his arms, carried her into the house, laid her down on the bed, and with a damp towel gently wiped the sand off her face.

✻

When he heard the horn of Mimì Augello's car, Montalbano helped Livia stand up and put her clothes in order. Utterly passive, she let him do as he wished. With an arm around her waist, he escorted her outside. Mimì did not get out of the car. He knew it was unwise to get too close to his superior; he might get bitten. He stared straight ahead the whole time, to avoid meeting the inspector's gaze. Right before getting in the car, Livia turned her head slightly and kissed Montalbano on the cheek. The inspector returned to the house, went into the bathroom, and got into the shower, clothes and all, turning the water on full blast. Then he swallowed two sleeping pills, which he never took, washed them down with a glass of whisky, threw himself on the bed, and waited for the inevitable blow to lay him out.

✻

When he woke it was five in the afternoon. He had a slight headache and felt nauseated.

'Augello here?' he asked, walking into the station.

Mimì entered Montalbano's office and prudently closed the door behind him. He looked resigned.

'If you start yelling like you usually do,' he said, 'it's probably better if we go outside.'

The inspector got up from his chair, brought himself face-to-face with Mimì, then put an arm around the other's neck.

'You're a real friend, Mimì. But I advise you to leave this room immediately. I'm liable to change my mind and start kicking you.'

*

'Inspector? Clementina Vasile Cozzo's on the line. Shall I put her through?'

'And who are you?'

It couldn't possibly be Catarella.

'What do you mean, who am I? I'm me.'

'And what the hell is your name?'

'It's Catarella, Chief! Poissonally in poisson!'

Thank God for that. The impromptu identity check had resuscitated the old Catarella, not the one the computer was inexorably transforming.

'Inspector! What happened? Are you angry with me?'

'Signora, believe me, I've had some pretty strange days...'

'You're forgiven. Could you come to my flat? I have something to show you.'

'Now?'

'Now.'

*

Signora Clementina escorted him into the living room and turned off the television.

'Look at this. It's the programme of tomorrow's concert, which Maestro Cataldo Barbera had someone bring to me a short while ago.'

Montalbano took the torn, squared notebook page from the signora's hand. Was this why she'd so urgently wanted to see him?

On it, in pencil, was written: *Friday, nine thirty. Concert in memory of Michela Licalzi.*

Montalbano gave a start. Did Maestro Barbera know the victim?

'That's why I asked you to come,' said Mrs Vasile Cozzo, reading the question in his eyes.

The inspector went back to studying the sheet of paper.

> Programme: G. Tartini, 'Variations on a Theme by Corelli'; J. S. Bach, 'Largo'; G. B. Viotti, from Concerto no. 24 in E minor.

He handed the sheet back to Mrs Vasile Cozzo.

'Did you know that they were acquainted, signora?'

'Never. And I wonder how that could be, since the Maestro never goes outside. As soon as I read that piece of paper, I knew it might be of interest to you.'

'I'm going to go upstairs and talk to him.'

'You're wasting your time. He'll refuse to see you. It's six thirty. He's already gone to bed.'

'What does he do, watch television?'

'He hasn't got a television, and he doesn't read news-papers. He goes to sleep, and then wakes up around two o'clock in the morning. I asked the maid if she knew why the Maestro keeps such odd hours, and she said she had no idea. But, after giving it some thought, I think I've found a plausible explanation.'

'Which is?'

'I believe that the Maestro, in so doing, blots out a specific period of time, that is, he cancels, skips over, the hours during which he normally used to perform. By sleeping through them, he erases them from his memory.'

'I see. But I can't not talk to him.'

'You could try tomorrow morning, after the concert.'

A door slammed upstairs.

'There,' said Mrs Vasile Cozzo, 'the maid is going home now.'

Montalbano made a move towards the door.

'Actually, Inspector, she's more a housekeeper than a maid,' Mrs Vasile Cozzo explained.

Montalbano opened the door. A woman in her sixties, appropriately dressed, descended the final steps from the floor above and greeted the inspector with a nod of the head.

'Ma'am, I'm Inspector—'

'I know.'

'I realize you're on your way home, and I don't want

to waste your time. But tell me, did Maestro Barbera and Mrs Licalzi know each other?'

'Yes. They met about two months ago. The lady had come to the Maestro on her own initiative. He was very happy about this, since he rather likes pretty women. They got into an involved conversation. I then brought them coffee, which they drank, and then they closed themselves in the studio, where you can't hear anything.'

'Soundproof?'

'Yes, sir. So he doesn't disturb the neighbours.'

'Did the lady ever come back?'

'Not when I was there.'

'And when are you there?'

'Can't you see? I leave in the evening.'

'Tell me something. If the Maestro has no television and doesn't read newspapers, how did he find out about the murder?'

'I told him myself, by chance, this afternoon. I saw the funeral announcement for tomorrow on the street.'

'And how did the Maestro react?'

'Very badly. He turned all pale and asked for his heart pills. What a fright I had! Anything else?'

SIXTEEN

That morning the inspector showed up at the office dressed in a grey suit, pale blue shirt, neutral tie and black shoes.

'My, my, don't we look fashionable?' said Mimì Augello.

Montalbano couldn't very well tell him he'd decked himself out to attend a violin recital at nine thirty in the morning. Mimì would have thought him insane. And rightly so, since the whole business did have something of the madhouse about it.

'Actually, I have to go to a funeral,' he muttered.

He went into his office; the phone was ringing.

'Salvo? This is Anna. A little while ago I got a phone call from Guido Serravalle.'

'Was he calling from Bologna?'

'No, from Montelusa. He said Michela'd given him my number some time ago. He knew we were friends. He's down here for the funeral, staying at the Della Valle.

He asked me to join him for lunch afterwards; he's going back in the afternoon. What should I do?'

'In what sense?'

'I don't know, I'm afraid I'll feel awkward.'

'Why?'

✶

'Inspector? This is Emanuele Licalzi. Are you coming to the funeral?'

'Yes. What time does it begin?'

'At eleven. When it's over, the hearse will head straight for Bologna after it leaves the church. Any news?'

'Nothing major, for now. Will you be staying long in Montelusa?'

'Till tomorrow morning. I need to talk to an estate agent about selling the house. I have to go there this afternoon with one of their representatives; they want to see it. By the way, yesterday evening I flew down here with Guido Serravalle. He's here for the funeral.'

'That must have been uncomfortable.'

'You think so?'

Dr Emanuele Licalzi had lowered his visor again.

✶

'Hurry, he's about to begin,' said Signora Clementina, leading him into the little parlour next to the living room. They sat down solemnly. For the occasion, the signora had put on an evening gown. She looked like one of

Boldini's ladies, only older. At nine thirty sharp, Maestro Barbera struck up the first notes. And before he'd been listening even five minutes, the inspector began to get a strange, disturbing feeling. It seemed to him as if the violin had suddenly become a voice, a woman's voice, that was begging to be heard and understood. Slowly but surely the notes turned into syllables, or rather into phonemes, and yet they expressed a kind of lament, a song of ancient suffering that at moments reached searing, mysteriously tragic heights. And this stirring female voice told of a terrible secret that could only be understood by someone capable of abandoning himself entirely to the sound, the waves of sound. He closed his eyes, profoundly shaken and troubled. But deep down he was also astonished. How could this violin have so changed in timbre since the last time he'd heard it? With eyes still closed, he let himself be guided by the voice. And he saw himself enter Michela Licalzi's house, walk through the living room, open the glass display, and pick up the violin case ... So *that*'s what had been tormenting him, the element that clashed with the whole! The blinding light that burst inside his head made him cry out.

'Were you also moved?' asked Signora Clementina, wiping away a tear. 'He's never played like that before.'

The concert must have ended at that very moment, for the signora plugged the phone back in, dialled the number, and applauded.

This time, instead of joining in, the inspector grabbed the phone.

'Maestro? Inspector Montalbano here. I absolutely have to speak to you.'

'And I to you.'

Montalbano hung up, and, in one swift motion, bent over, embraced Signora Clementina, kissed her forehead, and went out.

✲

The door to the flat was opened by the housekeeper.

'Would you like a coffee?'

'No, thank you.'

Cataldo Barbera came forward, hand extended.

On his way up the two flights of stairs, Montalbano had given some thought to how the Maestro might be dressed. He'd hit the nail on the head: Maestro Barbera, a tiny man with snow-white hair and small, black, but very intense eyes, was wearing a well-cut coat and tails.

The only jarring note was a white silk scarf wrapped around the lower part of his face, covering his nose, mouth and chin, leaving only his eyes and forehead exposed. The scarf was held in place by a gold hairpin.

'Please come in, make yourself comfortable,' Barbera said politely, leading him into the soundproof studio.

Inside, there was a glass display case with five violins; a complex stereo system; a set of metal office shelves stacked with CDs, LPs and cassette tapes; a bookcase, a desk and two armchairs. On the desk sat another violin, apparently the one the Maestro had just played in his recital.

'Today I used the Guarneri,' he said, confirming Montalbano's suspicion and gesturing towards the instrument. 'It has an incomparable voice, heavenly.'

Montalbano congratulated himself. Though he didn't know the first thing about music, he had nevertheless intuited that that violin sounded different from the one he'd heard in the previous recital.

'For a violinist, believe me, it's nothing short of a miracle to have such a jewel at one's disposal.' He sighed. 'Unfortunately, I have to give it back.'

'It's not yours?'

'I wish it were! The problem is, I no longer know whom to give it back to. I'd intended to phone the police station today and ask somebody there. But since you're here...'

'I'm at your service.'

'You see, that violin belonged to the late Mrs Licalzi.'

The inspector felt all his nerves tighten up like violin strings. If the Maestro had run his bow across him, a chord would have rung out.

'About two months ago,' Maestro Barbera recounted, 'I was practising with the window open. Mrs Licalzi, who happened to be walking by, heard me. She was very knowledgeable about music, you know. She saw my name on the intercom downstairs and wanted to meet me. She'd been at my very last performance in Milan, after which I retired, though nobody knew that at the time.'

'Why did you retire?'

The bluntness of the question caught the Maestro by surprise. He hesitated, though only for a moment, then pulled out the hairpin and slowly unwrapped the scarf. A monster: half his nose was gone; his upper lip had been entirely eaten away, exposing the gums.

'Is that a good enough reason?'

He wrapped the scarf around himself again, securing it with the pin.

'It's a very rare, degenerative form of lupus, totally incurable. How could I continue to appear in public?'

The inspector felt grateful to him for putting the scarf back on at once. He was impossible to look at; one felt horrified, nauseated.

'Anyway, that beautiful, gentle creature, talking of this and that, told me about a violin she'd inherited from a great-grandfather from Cremona who used to make stringed instruments. She added that, as a child, she'd heard it said within the family that it was worth a fortune, though she'd never paid much attention to this. These legends of priceless paintings and statuettes worth millions are common talk in families. I'm not sure why, but I became curious. A few days later she phoned me in the evening, then came round to pick me up, and took me to the house she'd recently built. The moment I saw that violin, I tell you, something burst inside me, I felt a kind of overpowering electrical shock. It was in a pretty bad state, but I knew it wouldn't take much to restore it to perfection. It was an Andrea Guarneri, Inspector, easily recognizable by the powerful glow of its amber-yellow varnish.'

The inspector glanced at the violin, and in all sincerity he didn't see any glow coming from it. Then again, he was hopeless in matters of music.

'I tried playing it,' said the Maestro, 'and for ten minutes I was transported to heaven in the company of Paganini, Ole Bull and others . . .'

'What's its market value?' asked the inspector, who usually flew close to the ground and had never come close to heaven.

'Market value?!' the Maestro said in horror. 'You can't put a price on an instrument like that!'

'All right, but if you had to quantify—'

'I really don't know . . . Two, three billion lire.'

Had he heard right? He had.

'I did make it clear to the lady that she mustn't risk leaving so valuable an instrument in a practically uninhabited house. We came up with a solution, also because I wanted authoritative confirmation of my assumption — that is, that it was indeed an Andrea Guarneri. She suggested I keep it here at my place. I didn't want to accept such an immense responsibility, but in the end she talked me into it, and she didn't even want a receipt. Then she drove me home and I gave her one of my violins to take its place in the old case. If anyone were to steal it, little harm would be done; it wasn't worth more than a few hundred thousand lire. The next morning I tried to reach a friend of mine in Milan, the foremost expert on violins there is. His secretary told me he was abroad, travelling the world, and wouldn't be back before the end of this month.'

'Please excuse me,' said the inspector. 'I'll be back shortly.'

He rushed out and ran all the way to headquarters on foot.

'Fazio!'

'At your service, Chief.'

Montalbano wrote something on a piece of paper, signed it and stamped it with the Vigàta Police seal to make it official.

'Come with me.'

They took his car and pulled up a short distance from the church.

'Give this note to Dr Licalzi. I want him to give you the keys to the house in Tre Fontane. I can't go in there myself. If I'm seen in church talking to the doctor, who's going to stop the rumours?'

Less than five minutes later they were already on their way to Tre Fontane.

They got out of the car, and Montalbano opened the front door. There was a foul, suffocating smell inside, owing not only to the lack of circulation, but also to the powders and sprays used by forensics.

With Fazio still behind him not asking any questions, he opened the glass display case, grabbed the violin case, went out, and relocked the door.

'Wait, I want to see something.'

He turned the corner of the house and went round to the back, which he'd never done the other times he'd been there. He found the rough draft of what would have one day become a vast garden. On the right, almost attached to the house, stood a giant sorb tree, the kind that produced little bright-red fruits rather sour in flavour, which Montalbano ate in great abundance when he was a child.

'I want you to climb up to the top branch.'

'Who, me?'

'No, your twin brother.'

Fazio started climbing half-heartedly. He was well into middle age and afraid of falling and breaking his neck.

'Wait for me there.'

'Yes, sir. After all, I was a Tarzan fan when I was a kid.'

Montalbano reopened the front door, went upstairs, turned on the bedroom light – here the smell grabbed him by the throat – and raised the rolling shutter without opening the window.

'Can you see me?' he yelled to Fazio.

'Yes, perfectly!'

He went out of the house, locked the door, and headed back to the car.

Fazio wasn't in it. He was still up in the tree, waiting for the inspector to tell him what to do next.

*

After dropping Fazio off in front of the church to give the keys back to Dr Licalzi ('Tell him we may need them again'), he drove to Maestro Barbera's place. There, he climbed the steps two at a time. The Maestro opened the door for him. He was now dressed in a turtleneck sweater and slacks, having doffed the coat and tails. The white silk scarf with gold pin, however, was still in place.

'Come in,' said Cataldo Barbera.

'No need, Maestro. I'll just be a few seconds. Is this the Guarneri's case?'

The Maestro took it, studied it closely, and handed it back.

'It certainly looks like it.'

Montalbano opened the case and, without taking the instrument out, asked, 'Is this the violin you gave to Michela to keep?'

The Maestro took two steps backward and extended his arm as if to shield himself from an unbearable sight.

'I wouldn't touch that thing with my little finger! Look at that! It's mass-produced! It's an affront to any proper violin!'

Here was confirmation of what the voice of the violin

had revealed to Montalbano. From the start he had unconsciously registered the difference between the container and its contents. It was clear even to him, who knew nothing about violins. Or about any other kind of instrument, for that matter.

'Among other things,' Cataldo Barbera continued, 'the one I gave to Michela Licalzi may have been of very modest value, but it rather looked like a Guarneri.'

'Thank you. I'll be seeing you.'

Montalbano started down the stairs.

'What should I do with the Guarneri?' the Maestro called out in a loud voice, still at sea, not having understood a thing.

'Just hang on to it for now. And play it as often as you can.'

*

They were loading the coffin into the hearse. Before the main portal of the church were many funeral wreaths lined up in a row. Emanuele Licalzi stood surrounded by a crowd of people expressing condolences. He looked unusually upset. Montalbano approached him and pulled him aside.

'I wasn't expecting all these people,' the doctor said.

'Your wife inspired a lot of affection. Did you get the keys back? I may have to ask you for them again.'

'I'm going to need them between four and five o'clock, to take the estate agent to the house.'

'I'll bear that in mind. Listen, Doctor, when you go into the house, you'll probably notice the violin is missing from the display case. That's because I took it. I'll return it to you this evening.'

The doctor looked dumbfounded.

'Is that of any relevance to the investigation? It's an utterly worthless object.'

'I need it for fingerprints,' Montalbano lied.

'In that case, don't forget that I held it in my hands when I showed it to you.'

'I won't forget. And, Doctor, one more thing, just for curiosity's sake: at what time did you leave Bologna yesterday evening?'

'I took the flight that leaves at six thirty, with a change at Rome, and arrived in Palermo at ten p.m.'

'Thanks.'

'Excuse me, Inspector, don't forget about the Twingo!'

Jesus, what a pain in the arse about that car!

*

Among the crowd of people already preparing to leave, he finally spotted Anna Tropeano talking to a tall, distinguished-looking man of about forty. It had to be Guido Serravalle. Then he noticed Giallombardo passing by on the street. He called to him.

'Where you going?'

'Home, Inspector, for lunch.'

'I'm very sorry, but you can't.'

'Christ, of all days you had to pick the day my wife made *pasta 'ncasciata.*'

'You'll eat it tonight. See those two over there? That brunette lady and the gentleman she's talking to?'

'Yessir.'

'Don't let the guy out of your sight. I'll be back at headquarters soon. Keep me posted every half hour. Everything he does, everywhere he goes.'

'Oh, all right,' said Giallombardo, resigned.

Montalbano left him and walked over to the pair. Anna, who hadn't seen him approaching, brightened at once. Apparently Serravalle's presence made her uncomfortable.

'Salvo, how are you?' She introduced them. 'Inspector Salvo Montalbano, Mr Guido Serravalle.'

Montalbano performed like a god.

'Of course, we already met over the phone!'

'Yes, I offered my help.'

'How could I forget? You came for the late Mrs Licalzi?'

'It was the least I could do.'

'Of course. Are you going back today?'

'Yes, I'll be leaving the hotel around five o'clock. I've got a flight out of Punta Ràisi at eight.'

'Good, good,' said Montalbano. He seemed happy that everyone was so happy and that, among other things, one could count on planes leaving on time.

'You know,' said Anna, assuming a nonchalant, worldly demeanour, 'Mr Serravalle was just inviting me to lunch. Why don't you join us?'

'I would love that,' said Serravalle, absorbing the blow.

A look of deep disappointment came over the inspector's face.

'If only I'd known earlier! I've got an appointment, alas.'

He held his hand out to Serravalle.

'Very pleased to have met you. However inappropriate it may seem to say so, given the circumstances.'

He was afraid he might be overdoing his perfect idiot act; the role was running away with him. Indeed, Anna was glaring at him with eyes that looked like two question marks.

'You and me, on the other hand, we'll talk later, eh, Anna?'

✻

In the doorway to headquarters he ran into Mimì, who was on his way out.

'Where are you off to?'

'To eat.'

'Jesus, is that all anyone can think of around here?'

'When it's time to eat, what else are we supposed to be thinking of?'

'Who've we got in Bologna?'

'As mayor?' asked Mimì, confused.

'What the fuck do I care who the mayor of Bologna is? Have we got any friends in their police department who can give us an answer in an hour's time?'

'Wait, there's Guggino, remember him?'

'Filiberto?'

'Right. He was transferred there a month ago. He's heading the immigration section.'

'Go and eat your spaghetti with clam sauce and all that Parmesan cheese on top,' Montalbano said by way of thanks, looking at him with contempt. How else could you look at someone with tastes like that?

*

It was 12.35. Hopefully Filiberto would still be in his office.

'Hello? Inspector Salvo Montalbano here. I'm calling from Vigàta. I'd like to speak with Filiberto Guggino.'

'Please hold.'

After a series of clicks he heard a cheerful voice.

'Salvo! Good to hear from you! How you doing?'

'Fine, Filibè. Sorry to bother you, but it's urgent. I need some answers within an hour, hour and a half at the most. I'm looking for a financial motive to a crime.'

'The only thing I have to waste is time.'

'I want you to tell me as much as you can possibly find out about someone who might be the victim of loan sharks – say, a businessman, heavy gambler...'

'That makes the whole thing a lot more difficult. I can

tell you who the loan sharks are, but not the people they've ruined.'

'Try anyway. Here's his name.'

*

'Chief? Giallombardo here. They're eating at the Contrada Capo restaurant, the one right on the sea. You know it?'

Unfortunately, yes, he did know it. He'd ended up there once by chance and had never forgotten it.

'Did they drive there separately?'

'No, they came in one car and he drove, so—'

'Don't let him out of your sight. I'm sure he's going to take the lady home, then go back to his hotel, the Della Valle. Keep me posted.'

*

Yes and no, the company that rented cars at Punta Ràisi Airport told him after humming and hawing for half an hour about not being authorized to give out information, so much so that he had to get the chief of airport police to intervene on his behalf. Yes, the previous evening, Thursday, that is, the gentleman in question had rented the car he was still using. And, no, the same gentleman had not rented a car from them on Wednesday evening of the previous week, according to the computer.

SEVENTEEN

Guggino's answer came a few minutes before three. It was long and detailed. Montalbano carefully took notes. Five minutes later Giallombardo phoned and told him Serravalle had gone back to his hotel.

'Stay right there and don't move,' the inspector ordered him. 'If you see him go out again before I've arrived, stop him with whatever excuse you can think of. Do a striptease or a belly dance, just don't let him leave.'

He quickly leafed through Michela's papers, remembering that he'd seen a boarding pass among them. There it was. It was for the last journey the woman would ever make from Bologna to Palermo. He put it in his pocket and called Gallo into his office.

'Take me to the Della Valle in the squad car.'

The hotel was halfway between Vigàta and Montelusa and had been built directly behind one of the most beautiful temples in the world – historical conservation offices, landscape constraints and zoning regulations be damned.

'Wait for me here,' the inspector said to Gallo when they got to the hotel. He then walked over to his own car. Giallombardo was taking a nap inside.

'I was sleeping with one eye open!' the policeman assured him.

The inspector opened the boot and took out the case with the cheap violin inside.

'You go back to the station,' he ordered Giallombardo.

He walked into the hotel lobby, looking exactly like a concert violinist.

'Is Mr Serravalle in?'

'Yes, he's in his room. Whom should I say?'

'You shouldn't say anything. You should only keep quiet. I'm Inspector Montalbano. And if you so much as pick up the phone, I'll run you in and we can talk about it later.'

'Fourth floor, room four sixteen,' said the receptionist, lips trembling.

'Has he had any phone calls?'

'I gave him his phone messages when he got in. There were three or four.'

'Let me talk to the operator.'

The operator, whom the inspector, for whatever reason, had imagined as a cute young woman, turned out to be an ageing, bald man in his sixties with glasses.

'The receptionist told me everything. About twelve a certain Eolo started calling from Bologna. He never left his last name. He called again about ten minutes ago and I forwarded the call to Mr Serravalle's room.'

*

In the lift, Montalbano pulled a list of the names of all those who on Wednesday evening of the previous week had rented cars at Punta Ràisi airport from his pocket. True, there was no Guido Serravalle; there was, however, one Eolo Portinari. And Guggino had told him this Portinari was a close friend of the antiquarian.

He tapped very lightly on the door, and as he was doing this, he remembered he'd left his pistol in the glove compartment.

'Come in, it's open.'

The antique dealer was lying down on the bed, hands behind his head. He'd taken off only his shoes and jacket; his tie was still knotted. As soon as he saw the inspector, he jumped to his feet like a jack-in-the-box.

'Relax, relax,' said Montalbano.

'But I insist!' said Serravalle, hastily slipping his shoes on. He even put his jacket back on. Montalbano had sat down in a chair, violin case on his knees.

'I'm ready. To what do I owe the honour?'

'The other day, when we spoke on the phone, you said you would make yourself available to me if I needed you.'

'Absolutely. I repeat the offer,' said Serravalle, also sitting down.

'I would have spared you the trouble, but since you came for the funeral, I thought I'd take advantage of the opportunity.'

'I'm glad. What do you want me to do?'

'Pay attention to me.'

'I'm sorry, I don't quite understand.'

'Listen to what I have to say. I want to tell you a story. If you think I'm exaggerating or wrong on any of the details, please interrupt and correct me.'

'I don't see how I could do that, Inspector, since I don't know the story you're about to tell me.'

'You're right. You mean you'll tell me your impressions at the end. The protagonist of my story is a gentleman who has a pretty comfortable life. He's a man of taste, owns a well-known antique shop, has a good clientele. It's a profession our protagonist inherited from his father.'

'Excuse me,' said Serravalle, 'what is the setting of your story?'

'Bologna,' said Montalbano. He continued, 'Sometime during the past year, roughly speaking, this gentleman meets a young woman from the upper-middle class. They become lovers. Their relationship is risk free. The woman's husband, for reasons that would take too long to explain here, turns not a blind eye, as they say, but two blind eyes on their affair. The lady still loves her husband, but is very attached, sexually, to her lover.'

He stopped short.

'May I smoke?' Montalbano asked.

'Of course,' said Serravalle, pushing an ashtray closer to him.

Montalbano took the packet out slowly, extracted three cigarettes, rolled them one by one between his thumb and forefinger, opted for the one that seemed softest to him, put the other two back in the packet, then started patting himself in search of his lighter.

'Sorry I can't help you, I don't smoke,' said the antique dealer.

The inspector finally found the lighter in the breast pocket of his jacket, studied it as if he'd never seen it before, lit the cigarette, and put the lighter back in his pocket.

Before starting to speak, he looked wild-eyed at Serravalle. The antiquarian's upper lip was moist; he was beginning to sweat.

'Where was I?'

'The woman was very attached to her lover.'

'Oh, yes. Unfortunately, our protagonist has a very nasty vice. He gambles, and gambles big. Three times in the last three months he's been caught in illegal gambling dens. One day, just imagine, he ends up in hospital, brutally beaten. He claims he was assaulted and robbed, but the police suspect, I say *suspect*, it was a warning to pay up old gambling debts. In any event, the situation for our protagonist, who keeps on gambling and losing, gets worse and worse. He confides in his girlfriend, and she tries to help him as best she can. Sometime before, she'd had this idea to build a house in Sicily, because she liked the place. Now this house turns out to be a perfect opportunity because, by inflating her costs, she can funnel hundreds of millions of lire to her boyfriend. She plans to build a garden, probably even a swimming pool: new sources of diverted money. But it turns out to be a drop in the ocean, hardly two or three hundred million. One day, this woman, who, for the sake of convenience, I'll call Michela—'

'Wait a second,' Serravalle broke in with a snicker that was supposed to be sardonic. 'And your protagonist, what's his name?'

'Let's say ... Guido,' said Montalbano, as if this were a negligible detail.

Serravalle grimaced. The sweat was now making his shirt stick to his chest.

'You don't like that? We can call them Paolo and Francesca, if you like. The essence remains the same.'

He waited for Serravalle to say something, but since he didn't open his mouth, Montalbano continued.

'One day, Michela, in Vigàta, meets a famous violin soloist who has retired there. They take a liking to each other, and Michela tells him about an old violin she inherited from her great-grandfather. Just for fun, I think, she shows it to the Maestro, and he, upon seeing it, realizes he's in the presence of an instrument of tremendous value, both musically and monetarily. A couple of billion lire, at least. When Michela returns to Bologna, she tells her lover the whole story. If what the Maestro told her is true, they can easily sell the violin, since Michela's husband has only seen it once or twice, and nobody is aware of its real value. All they have to do is replace it with any old violin, and Guido's troubles will be over for ever.'

Montalbano stopped talking, drummed on the case with his fingers, and sighed.

'Now comes the worst part,' he said.

'Well,' said Serravalle, 'you can tell me the rest another time.'

'I could, but then I'd have to make you come back here from Bologna or else go there myself. Too much trouble. But since you're polite enough to listen to me, even though you're dying of the heat in here, I'll explain to you why I consider this the worst part.'

'Because you'll have to talk about a murder?'

Montalbano looked at the antique dealer, mouth agape.

'You think that's why? No, I'm accustomed to murder. I consider it the worst part because I have to leave the realm of concrete fact and venture into a man's mind, enter his thoughts. A novelist would have the road laid out in front of him, but I'm simply a reader of what I think are good books. Excuse me for digressing. At this point our protagonist gathers some information on the Maestro whom Michela spoke to him about. And he discovers that not only is he a great performer of inter-national renown, but also a connoisseur of the history of the instrument he plays. In short, there's a ninety-nine per cent chance his hunch is right on target. There is no question, however, that, if left in Michela's hands, the matter will take for ever to settle. Not only will she want to sell the instrument, well, quietly, yes, but also legally, so of those two billion lire, after sundry expenses, commissions and the workings of our government, which will swoop down from above like a highwayman, she'll be left in the end with less than a billion. But there's a shortcut. And our protagonist thinks about it day and night. He talks about it with a friend. This friend, whom we'll call, say, Eolo...'

It had gone well for him; conjecture had become certainty. As though struck by a large-calibre bullet, Serravalle abruptly stood up from his chair only to fall heavily back down in it. He undid the knot of his tie.

'Yes, let's call him Eolo. Eolo agrees with the protagonist that there's only one way: eliminate the lady and seize the violin, replacing it with another of little value. Serravalle persuades him to give him a hand. Most importantly, theirs is a secret friendship, perhaps based on gambling, and Michela has never seen Eolo before. On the appointed day, they take the last flight out of Bologna together, changing at Rome for the connecting flight to Palermo. Now, Eolo Portinari—'

Serravalle gave a start, but feebly, as when a dying man is shot a second time.

'How silly of me, I gave him a last name! Anyway,

Eolo Portinari is travelling without luggage, or almost, whereas Guido brings along a large suitcase. Aboard the plane, the two men pretend not to know each other. Shortly before flying out of Rome, Guido phones Michela, telling her he's on his way down. He says he needs her and she should come and pick him up at Punta Ràisi airport. Maybe he gets her to think he's fleeing his creditors, who want to kill him. Landing in Palermo, Guido heads to Vigàta with Michela, while Eolo rents a car and also heads to Vigàta, though at a safe distance. During the drive, the protagonist probably tells his girlfriend that his life was in danger if he remained in Bologna. He'd come up with the idea of hiding out for a few days at Michela's new house. Who would ever think of looking for him down there? The woman, happy to have her lover with her, accepts the idea. Before they get to Montelusa, she stops at a bar, buys two sandwiches and a bottle of mineral water. But as she's doing this, she stumbles on a stair and falls, and Serravalle is seen by the owner of the bar. They arrive at Michela's house after midnight. Michela immediately takes a shower and runs into her man's arms. They make love once, and then her lover asks her if they can do it a special way. And at the end of this second coupling, he presses her face into the mattress, suffocating her. And do you know why he asked Michela to do it that way? No doubt they'd done it before, but at that moment, he didn't want his victim to look at him as he was killing her. Right after he's committed the murder, he hears a kind of moan outside, a muffled cry. He goes to the window and sees, in a tree right next to the house, illuminated by the light from the window, a Peeping Tom, or so he thinks, who has just witnessed the murder. Still naked, the protagonist rushes outside, grabbing some sort of weapon along the way, and strikes the stranger in the face with it, though the intruder manages to escape. But our protagonist hasn't got a minute to lose. He gets dressed, opens up the display case, grabs the violin, and puts it in his suitcase. From this same suitcase he pulls out the cheap violin and puts this in the old violin's case. A few minutes later, Eolo comes by in his car and the protagonist gets in. What they do next is of no importance. The following morning they're at Punta Ràisi to take the first flight for Rome. Up to this point everything has gone well for our protagonist, who makes sure to keep track of developments by reading the Sicilian newspapers. Things begin to go even better when he learns that the murderer has been found and that he actually had enough time to admit his guilt before being killed in a gun battle. The protagonist realizes there's no longer any need to wait before putting the violin up for sale on the black market, and so he turns it over to Eolo Portinari, who will try to make a deal. But then a new complication arises. The protagonist learns the case has been re-opened. He jumps at the opportunity to go to the funeral and races down to Vigàta so he can talk to Michela's friend Anna, the only friend he knows and the only person who might be able to tell him how things stand. After talking to her, he goes back to his hotel. And here he receives a phone call from Eolo: it turns out the violin is only worth a few hundred thousand lire. The protagonist realizes he's fucked. He killed someone for nothing.'

'Therefore,' said Serravalle, who was so drenched in sweat he looked as if he'd washed his face without drying it, 'your protagonist stumbled into that tiny margin of error, that one per cent, he'd granted the Maestro.'

'When you're unlucky at gambling...' was the inspector's comment.

'Something to drink?'

'No, thank you.'

Serravalle opened his minibar, took out three little bottles of whisky, poured them straight into a glass without ice, and drank it all down in two gulps.

'It's an interesting story, Inspector. You suggested I give you my impressions at the end, and now, if you don't mind, I'll do just that. To begin. Your protagonist wouldn't have been so stupid as to fly under his own name, would he?'

Montalbano inched the boarding pass a little out of his jacket pocket, just enough for the other to see it.

'No, Inspector, that's useless. Assuming a boarding pass exists, it means nothing, even if the protagonist's name is on it. Anyone can use it, since they don't ask for ID. As for the encounter at the bar ... You say it was night, and a matter of a few seconds. Admit it, any identification would be unreliable.'

'Your reasoning holds,' said the inspector.

'To continue. Let me offer a variant of your story. The protagonist mentions his girlfriend's discovery to a man named Eolo Portinari, a two-bit hood. And Portinari comes to Vigàta on his own initiative and does everything you say your protagonist did. Portinari rents the car, using his driver's licence, Portinari tries to sell the violin that so dazzled the Maestro, and Portinari rapes the woman so the murder will look like a crime of passion.'

'Without ejaculating?'

'Of course! The semen would have made it easy to trace the DNA!'

Montalbano raised two fingers, as if asking permission to go to the bathroom.

'I'd like to say a couple of things about your observations. You're absolutely right. Proving the protagonist's guilt will be long and arduous, but not impossible. Therefore, from this moment on, the protagonist will have two vicious dogs at his heels, his creditors and the police. The second thing is that the Maestro wasn't wrong in his estimate of the violin's value. It is indeed worth two billion lire.'

'But just now . . .'

Serravalle realized he was giving himself away and immediately fell silent. Montalbano went on as if he hadn't heard.

'My protagonist is very crafty. Just imagine, he keeps phoning the hotel, asking for his girlfriend, even after he's killed her. But there's one detail he's unaware of.'

'What's that?'

'Look, the story's so far-fetched that I've half a mind not to tell you.'

'Make an effort.'

'I don't feel like it – oh, all right, just as a favour to you. My protagonist found out from Michela that the Maestro's name is Cataldo Barbera, and he did a lot of research on him. Now, give the hotel operator a ring and ask him to phone Maestro Barbera, whose number's in the phone book. Tell him you're calling on my behalf, and have him tell you the story himself.'

Serravalle stood up, picked up the receiver, told the operator who he wanted to talk to. He remained on the line.

'Hello? Is this Maestro Barbera?'

As soon as the other replied, Serravalle hung up.

'I'd rather hear you tell it.'

'OK. Michela brings the Maestro to her house in her car, late one evening. As soon as Cataldo Barbera sees the violin, he practically faints. Then he plays it, and there can be no more doubt: it's a Guarneri. He talks about this with Michela, and tells her he wants to have it examined by a certified expert. At the same time he advises her not to leave the instrument in a seldom-inhabited house. So

Michela entrusts the violin to the Maestro, who takes it home and in exchange gives her one of his violins to put in the case. The one which my protagonist, knowing nothing, proceeds to steal. Ah, I forgot: my protagonist, after killing the woman, also filches her bag with her jewels and Piaget watch inside. How does the expression go? Every little bit helps. He also makes off with her clothes and shoes, but this is merely to muddy the waters a little more and to thwart the DNA tests.'

Montalbano was ready for anything, except Serravalle's reaction. At first it seemed to him that the antiquarian, who had turned his back to him to look out the window, was crying. Then the man turned around and Montalbano realized he was trying very hard to refrain from laughing. But all it took was that split second in which his eyes met the inspector's to make the man's laughter burst forth in all its violence. Serravalle was laughing and crying at once. Then, with a visible effort, he calmed down.

'Maybe it's better if I come with you,' he said.

'I advise you to do so,' said Montalbano. 'The people waiting for you in Bologna have other things in mind for you.'

'Let me put a few things in my bag and we can go.'

Montalbano saw him bend over a small suitcase that was on a bench. Something in Serravalle's movement disturbed him and he sprang to his feet.

'No!' the inspector shouted, leaping forward.

Too late. Guido Serravalle had put the barrel of a revolver in his mouth and pulled the trigger. Barely suppressing his nausea, the inspector wiped away the warm, viscous matter that was dripping down his own face.

EIGHTEEN

Half of Guido Serravalle's head was gone. The blast inside the small hotel room had been so loud that Montalbano heard a kind of buzz in his ears. How was it possible that nobody had yet come knocking on the door to ask what had happened? The Hotel Della Valle had been built in the late nineteenth century and had thick, solid walls. Maybe at that hour all the foreigners were out amusing themselves taking pictures of the temples. So much the better.

The inspector went into the bathroom, washed his sticky, bloodied hands as best he could, and picked up the phone.

'Inspector Montalbano here. There's a police car in your car park. Tell the officer to come up here. And please send the manager immediately.'

The first to arrive was Gallo. The moment he saw his superior with blood on his face and clothes, he got scared.

'Chief, Chief! You hurt?'

'Calm down, it's not my blood. It's that guy's.'

'Who's that?'

'Mrs Licalzi's murderer. But for the moment, don't say anything to anybody. Hurry into Vigàta and have Augello send out an all-points bulletin to Bologna, telling them to be on the lookout for a shady character named Eolo Portinari. I'm sure they've already got the facts on him. He's his accomplice,' he concluded, gesturing at the suicide. 'And listen. Come straight back here when you're done.'

Gallo, at the door, stepped aside to let in the hotel manager, a giant at least six and a half feet tall and of comparable girth. When he saw the corpse with half a head and the room in disarray the manager said, 'What?' as if he hadn't understood a question, dropped to his knees in slow motion, then fell face forward on the floor, out cold. The manager's reaction had been so immediate that Gallo hadn't had time to leave. Together they dragged the colossus into the bathroom, propped him up against the edge of the bath, whereupon Gallo took the shower extension, turned on the water, and aimed it at his head. The man came to almost at once.

'What luck! What luck!' he mumbled while drying himself off.

As Montalbano gave him a questioning look, the manager confirmed what the inspector had been thinking, and explained, 'The Japanese group are all out for the day.'

✲

Before Judge Tommaseo, Dr Pasquano, the new captain of the Flying Squad and the forensics team got there, Montalbano was forced to change out of his suit and shirt, having yielded to the pressures of the hotel manager, who insisted on lending him some of his own things. He could have fitted twice into the giant's clothes. With his hands lost in the sleeves, and the trousers gathered like accordions over his shoes, he looked like Bagonghi the dwarf. And this put him in a far worse mood than the fact of having repeatedly to describe, each time from the top, the details of his finding the killer and then witnessing his suicide. Between all the questions and answers, observations and explanations, the yeses, nos, buts and howevers, he wasn't free to return to the Vigàta – to the station, that is – until almost eight o'clock that evening.

'Have you shrunk?' asked Mimì upon seeing him.

By the skin of his teeth he managed to dodge the punch Montalbano threw at him, which would have broken his nose.

＊

There was no need for the inspector to say 'Everybody in my office!' since they all came in of their own accord. And he gave them the satisfaction they deserved, explaining, in minute detail, how the clouds of suspicion first came to gather over Serravalle and how he met his tragic end. The most intelligent observation was made by Mimì Augello.

'It's a good thing he shot himself. It would have been

hard to keep him in jail without any concrete proof. A good lawyer could have sprung him in no time.'

'But the guy killed himself!' said Fazio.

'So what?' Mimì retorted. 'It was the same with that poor Maurizio Di Blasi. Who can say he didn't come out of the cave with his shoe in his hand in the hope that they'd shoot him down, which they did, thinking it was a weapon?'

'In fact, Inspector, why was he shouting he wanted to be punished?' asked Germanà.

'Because he'd witnessed the murder and hadn't been able to prevent it,' Montalbano concluded.

While the others were filing out of his office, he remembered something, and he knew that if he didn't get it taken care of at once, by the following day he was liable to have forgotten about it entirely.

'Gallo, listen. I want you to go down to our garage, get all the papers that are in the Twingo, and bring them up here to me. Also, talk to our chief mechanic and have him draw up an estimate for repairs. Then, if he's interested in selling it, tell him to go ahead.'

*

'Chief, hear me out for jest a minute?'

'Come on in, Cat.'

Catarella was red in the face, embarrassed and happy.

'What's the matter? Talk.'

'Got my report card for the first week, Chief. The

course runs from Monday to Friday morning. I wanted to show it to you.'

It was a sheet of paper folded in two. All A's. Under the heading 'Observations', the instructor had written, 'He was first in the class.'

'Well done, Catarella! You're the pride of the department!'

Catarella nearly started crying.

'How many are there in your class?'

'Amato, Amoroso, Basile, Bennato, Bonura, Catarella, Cimino, Farinella, Filippone, Lo Dato, Scimeca and Zìcari. That makes twelve, Chief. If I had my computer here, I'd a done it faster.'

Montalbano put his head in his hands.

Was there a future for humanity?

*

Gallo returned from his visit to the Twingo.

'I talked to the mechanic. Said he'd take care of selling it. In the glove compartment I found the registration card and a road map.'

He set it all down on the inspector's desk, but didn't leave. He looked even more uneasy than Catarella.

'What's the matter?'

Without answering, Gallo handed him a little rectangle of heavy paper.

'I found this on the front seat, passenger's side.'

It was a boarding pass for Punta Ràisi airport, 10 p.m.

The date on the stub corresponded to Wednesday of the previous week, and passenger's name was G. Spina. Why, Montalbano asked himself, did people always use their real initials when assuming a false name? Guido Serravalle had lost his boarding pass in Michela's car. After the murder, he hadn't had the time to look for it, or else he thought he still had it in his pocket. That was why, when speaking of it, he had denied its existence and even mentioned the possibility that the passenger hadn't used his real name. But with the stub now in Montalbano's hand, they could have traced the ticket back, however laboriously, to the person who actually did take that flight. Only then did he realize that Gallo was still standing in front of his desk, a dead-serious expression on his face.

'If we'd only looked inside the car first . . .'

Indeed. If only they'd searched the Twingo the day after the body was found, the investigation would have taken the right path. Maurizio would still be alive and the real murderer would be in jail. If only . . .

*

It had all been, from the start, one mistake after another. Maurizio was mistaken for a murderer, the shoe was mistaken for a weapon, one violin was mistaken for another, and this one mistaken for a third. And Serravalle wanted to be mistaken for someone named Spina . . . Just past the bridge, he stopped the car, but did not get out. The lights were on in Anna's house; he sensed she was expecting him. He lit a cigarette, but halfway through he flicked it out of the window, put the car back in gear, and left.

It wasn't a good idea to add another mistake to the list.

＊

He entered his house, slipped out of the clothes that made him look like Bagonghi the dwarf, opened the refrigerator, took out ten or so olives, and cut himself a slice of caciocavallo cheese.

He went and sat outside on the veranda. The night was luminous, the sea slowly churning. Not wanting to waste any more time, he got up and dialled the number.

'Livia? It's me. I love you.'

'What's wrong?' asked Livia, alarmed.

In the whole time they'd been together, Montalbano had only told her he loved her at difficult, even dangerous, moments.

'Nothing. I'm busy tomorrow morning; I have to write a long report for the commissioner. Barring any complications, I'll hop on a plane in the afternoon and come.'

'I'll be waiting for you,' said Livia.

Author's Note

This fourth investigation of Inspector Montalbano (of which the names, places and situations have been invented out of whole cloth) involves violins. Like his character, the author is not qualified to talk or write about musical instruments (for a while, to the despair of the neighbours, he attempted to study the tenor sax). Therefore all pertinent information has been culled from books on the violin by S. F. Sacconi and F. Farga.

I also express my gratitude to Dr Silio Bozzi, who saved me from falling into a few technical errors in recounting the investigation.

Notes

page 16 – **face that he hid under a Belfiore martyr's moustache and beard** – The *martiri di Belfiore* were Italian patriots executed by the Austrians between 1851 and 1854 in the Belfiore Valley outside of Mantua in northern Italy during the early phases of Risorgimento, the Italian struggle for unification and independence from foreign occupiers. Inspired by a clergyman, Don Enrico Tazzoli, who met the same end, the 'martyrs' all wore moustaches and full beards, and their hirsute faces are a familiar sight in Italian textbooks.

page 29 – **'Pippo Baudo'** – A famous Italian television personality and MC of variety shows.

page 35 – **that more famous Nicolò Tommaseo** – Niccolò Tommaseo (b. Srebrenica, 1802 d. Florence, 1874) was a well-known Italian philologist and man of letters, author of, among other things, *Dictionary of Synonyms* and *Comment on the Divine Comedy*, and editor of a collection of Balkan folk songs and tales. A liberal Catholic by belief, he was a member of the provisional Venetian Republican government constituted in 1848 in defiance of the Austrian occupation. The original text of the Manzoni quote, in Lombard dialect, is '*Sto Tommaseo ch'eg gha on pè in sagrestia e vun in casìn.*'

page 36 – **He was a raven to boot** – In Italian, a person who enjoys bearing bad news is called a *corvo* (raven or crow).

page 37 – **given the government in power at that moment, and the fact that the Free Channel always leaned to the left** – Italy at the time was still being governed by a centre-left coalition.

page 50 – **'goes around with half a billion in her bag'** – At the time of the novel's writing (1996–7) half a billion lire was worth about £172,000.

page 52 – **side dish of gentle *tinnirùme*** – *Tinnirùme* are gently steamed flower tops of long courgettes.

page 58 – **'from Punta Ràisi to Bologna'** – Punta Ràisi is the airport serving the greater metropolitan area of Palermo and gets its name from the headland where it is located.

page 67 – **'I teach at the *liceo scientifico* of Montelusa'** – Italian secondary schools are called *licei*. There exist three different kinds of *liceo*: *liceo scientifico*, emphasizing scientific studies; *liceo classico*, emphasizing humanistic studies; and *liceo artistico*, emphasizing the arts. Students are grouped according to natural proclivities and personal preferences.

page 83 – **'Half a million lire'** – About £172.

page 90 – **prepared the *napoletana*** – A *napoletana* is an old-fashioned, usually tin espresso pot that one turns upside down at the first moment of boiling, allowing the hot water to filter down through the coffee grounds by force of gravity. The coffee thus obtained is judged to be superior to that created when the water is forced up at full boil through the grounds.

page 109 – '**Azione Cattolica**' – A Catholic youth organization disbanded during the Fascist era and reconstituted after World War II.

page 109 – *Famiglia Cristiana* ... *L'Osservatore Romano* – *Famiglia Cristiana* is a weekly magazine published by the Catholic Church. *L'Osservatore Romano* is the daily newspaper of the Vatican.

page 111 – '**Ah, these repenters!**' – Montalbano is referring ironically to the so-called *pentiti* ('repenters'), Mafia turncoats who turn state's evidence and are then treated very leniently, and practically coddled, by the government. See A. Camilleri, *The Snack Thief* (Macmillan, 2003).

page 114 – **it was called La Cacciatora. Naturally, they had no game** – *La Cacciatora* means 'the huntress'.

page 114 – **a hefty serving of delicious** *caponata* – *Caponata* is a zesty traditional southern Italian appetizer usually made up of sautéed aubergine, tomato, green pepper, garlic, onion, celery, black olives, vinegar, olive oil and anchovies.

page 114 – '**A joyous start is the best of guides**' – In Italian: '*Principio sì giolivo ben conduce.*' Matteo Maria Boiardo (1441–94), *Orlando Innamorato*.

page 119 – *tetù, taralli, viscotti regina* **and Palermitan** *mostaccioli* – These are all varieties of hard Italian *biscotti*. *Tetù* and *taralli* are covered with sugar but vary in size; *viscotti regina* are covered with sesame seeds; and Palermitan *mostaccioli* are made out of dough soaked in mulled wine.

page 119 – **a colourful** *cassata* – A traditional Sicilian sponge cake filled with sweetened ricotta, candied fruit, raisins, pine nuts, pistachios and jam, usually apricot. Not to be confused with the ice cream of the same name, which has some of the same ingredients.

page 123 – **Aldo Gagliardo ... as hale and hearty as his name** – Gagliardo means 'strong, vigorous, robust'.

page 166 – **a gigantic Saracen olive tree** – The *ulivo saraceno* is a very ancient olive tree with gnarled trunk, tangled branches and very long roots. The name suggests that the tree dates from the time of the Arab conquest of Sicily (ninth to eleventh centuries).

page 168 – **'Di Blasi doesn't have a licence to carry a gun, nor has he ever reported owning any weapons'** – In Italy, there are two kinds of firearms permits. The first is the licence to carry a gun, whether a pistol or rifle. With the second, one may only keep the firearm at home.

page 169 – **baby octopus *alla luciana*** – In this simple dish, the octopi are cooked in a spicy tomato sauce with garlic and hot pepper.

page 207 – **five million lire** – About £1,720.

page 207 – **one hundred and fifteen million lire** – About £41,000.

page 222 – **like one of Boldini's ladies** – Giovanni Boldini (1845–1931) was a cosmopolitan Italian painter originally from Ferrara who spent much of his career in Paris. A friend of both Whistler and Sargent, he was greatly influenced by the French painting of the period. He is best known for his portraits of characters from Parisian high society and the artistic milieu.

page 226 – 'Two, three billion lire' – Roughly between £690,000 and £1,000,000.

page 227 – 'a few hundred thousand lire' – A hundred or so pounds.

page 236 – The hotel ... zoning regulations be damned – Outside the Sicilian city of Agrigento, Camilleri's model for the city of Montelusa, stands the Greek Temple of Concord (440 BC, named retroactively), by far the best preserved of the ruins in this so-called Valley of Temples. In the modern age, against the protests of conservationists, historians and people of good sense, a large, unsightly hotel was built directly behind the archaeological site, right on the boundary line designating the perimeter beyond which it is now illegal to build – a demarcation determined only *after* the hotel was erected.

page 253 – Bagonghi the dwarf – Bagonghi was a famous Italian dwarf who performed as a clown in circuses all over Europe and often wore clothes that were far too big for him.

Notes compiled by Stephen Sartarelli